Bryce ran a finger down the other initials. 'The supermarket manager's on his second warning. So are the security man and the greengrocer. Our pal the ticket tout had to be nudged firmly on Tuesday night – we had a job findin' him, I think he's bein' chased by other people. I'll keep a close watch on him from now on. The bloke from the DHSS is due to fall off his bus on the way home tomorrow night – he's been sliding back very badly on the payments – ' Bryce looked up. 'That leaves the fadin' rock star.'

Sid nodded. 'Simon Wicks. It's a pity about him. He seemed like a good bet . . .'

By the same author

The Outsider
The Dark Side of the Sun

EastEnders Novels

Home Fires Burning
Swings and Roundabouts
Good Intentions
The Flower of Albert Square
Blind Spots
Hopes and Horizons
The Baffled Heart
Growing Wild
A Place in Life
A Single Man
Taking Chances

HUGH MILLER

Elbow Room

EastEnders – Book 12

By arrangement with the
British Broadcasting Corporation

GRAFTON BOOKS
A Division of the Collins Publishing Group

LONDON GLASGOW
TORONTO SYDNEY AUCKLAND

Grafton Books
A Division of the Collins Publishing Group
8 Grafton Street, London W1X 3LA

A Grafton Paperback Original 1988

ISBN 0-586-07229-2

Printed and bound in Great Britain by
Collins, Glasgow
Set in Times 03008283

Tuesday

The first day of October, misty with a colder breeze than lately, and already a few of the lunchtime punters had said this was it, the start of autumn, the beginning of the nice golden slide into winter. The way Wicksy saw it, this was the real start of the rot. Everything on his personal horizon was composting. No new growth, only decline and decay.

'You look like you lost a quid an' found ten pee,' Jacko said. They were cleaning up the tables after closing.

'It's more like I got rid of a headache an' caught leprosy,' Wicksy said, stacking ashtrays. 'Don't worry about me. I'll pull through.'

If only he could believe it.

'You've got a broody face on, that's what I was wonderin' about.'

'There's no life without a few woes, Jacko.'

He needed a sign, a good one. He needed proof that miracles could happen for the likes of him. But it didn't do to let people like Jacko know the score. Jacko didn't like trouble on his premises. If a barman had big problems, Jacko preferred him to have them some place else. The last thing Wicksy needed was to lose this job.

'Got time to do some bottlin' up before you go, Simon?'

Wicksy nodded. 'Sure.' Anything to keep himself off the streets and away from threat. 'I was goin' to offer, as a matter of fact.'

'Ah, you're a good bloke.' Jacko pressed the bottom of his spine with both hands and grunted. 'My back's givin' me gyp. The doc says I need to lose weight, but I don't know – I tried it once before. Felt bloody miserable for weeks on end an' my back got no better.' He patted his soft belly. 'I reckon I'll hang on to my appetite an' let other people do the heavy work.'

'Well – now you're gettin' on a bit, it's the thing to do anyway. Delegate. Sit back an' enjoy your twilight years.'

'Cheeky bugger.' Jacko hoisted a chair on to a table and winced. 'You'll be fifty yourself one day.'

Wicksy wished it was now. Fifty, with all the trouble well behind him.

'How's things with you an' that Beckie?' Jacko said. 'Givin' you any back trouble, is she?'

'Everythin's just fine thanks, Jacko. My back's holdin' up a treat.'

Among his other traits Jacko was inclined to keep a paternal eye on his younger staff, especially in the area of their off-duty relationships. Wicksy was never sure if it was genuine interest with a touch of concern, or a less-than-wholesome preoccupation with other people's sex lives. A bit of both, maybe.

'Just watch you don't get yourself trapped into nothin',' Jacko went on. 'Some of these little girls are good at leadin' a bloke along by the nose an' keepin' him sweet, until he hears the gates clangin' shut behind him.'

'Beckie's not like that. She's all on the surface. No schemin'.'

'That's what I used to think about my missus,' Jacko said glumly. 'Twenty-three years of supportin' her an her expensive habits, that's what I got for bein' gullible. Then at the end of it she waltzes off on the arm of a piggin' Greek with a great line of patter an' a motor-drive in his backside.'

The story was well-known in that part of Ilford. Five

6

years ago Jacko's wife, Alice, had fallen for Alexiou, a smouldery-eyed, sideburned charmer who had a meat-packing business somewhere in South London and regularly did business with a retail outlet near Jacko's pub, the Ginger Giant. In a matter of weeks Alice was spending her nights off with Alexiou, taking no care at all to keep neighbours and customers from knowing what she was up to. As can happen in such affairs, the husband was the last to know. One morning, two months after Alexiou had appeared on the scene, Jacko woke to find his wife and a substantial chunk of their savings gone. His bewilderment was taken care of by a neighbour, who pointed out she was only telling him for his own peace of mind. A few days later he was filled in even further when Alice wrote to explain she had set up home with her Greek and would be suing for divorce on the grounds that the marriage had broken down – irretrievably, of course. Jacko sighed, resigned himself, and proceeded thereafter to lavish all his concern on his bar staff and his ailing spine.

'I don't have any plans for gettin' married,' Wicksy said as he hauled three stacked crates of bottled ale into position by the shelves behind the bar. 'It's all right for some people, I suppose. But not me. I need to expand. I need elbow room for my plans and my ideas, know what I mean? A wife cramps a bloke.'

'Yeah, well. Try to keep thinkin' that way an' you'll be all right.' Jacko paused, watching Wicksy. 'If it's not girl trouble you've got, what is it?'

Wicksy tried to look puzzled.

'You admitted a minute ago you're feelin' rough. What's up?'

There was always the temptation to tell Jacko to mind his own business. But for someone who valued his job, it

7

was wisest to keep it at the level of temptation and never given in to the impulse to tell the guv'nor he was a nosey old git.

'It's my Mum,' Wicksy lied.

'Oh, I see.' Everything was now clear to Jacko. 'What's our Pat been up to now, then?'

He could take his pick, Wicksy thought. Pat's way of life was another well-known story around Ilford. It had stopped embarrassing Wicksy years ago.

'She got shirty with a bloke from the council a couple of days ago. She'd been complainin' about the outside loo not workin' an' finally they had a look an' decided the damage was down to her. They'd repair it, the official said, but she'd have to pay. So Mum said that was a dead liberty an' she was goin' to take her complaint higher. The bloke was daft enough to tell her she could take it as high as she liked. So she slanged him a bit, an' he defended himself with a bit of slang of his own. The upshot was Mum belted him one an' the law got called in.'

'Nothin' changes much,' Jacko said wearily. 'Best you can do, Simon, is put it out of your mind. Worryin' won't make no difference. Pat's set in her ways. I know that as well as most.'

For two and a half years, until late 1982, Pat had done a regular three-nights-a-week stint behind Jacko's public bar. It had been a wearing time for Jacko and three years later he still talked about it. There had been cases of customers being insulted, others being outrageously chatted-up, others cheated on their change. With any other employee instant dismissal would have followed a single breach, let alone the dozens committed by Pat. But she had a way of casting doubt even on the clearest-cut case. Time and again Jacko found himself compromising and,

8

in the end, giving Pat the benefit of the doubt. She had finally been sacked for getting so drunk on duty one night that she fell across a table, demolishing six drinks and ruining a sports jacket and two pairs of trousers. Her powers of persuasive chat might have retrieved her from even that catastrophe, except that she promptly started a stand-up clawing-match with a woman who'd called her a drunken old cow.

'Where's she livin' these days, anyway?' Jacko said. 'Still in the council house down Dover Road?'

'That's right.' Wicksy set aside an empty crate and started on another one. 'She's been near gettin' flung out of there for as long as I can remember, but she manages to hold on.'

'An' you've been stayin' there with her, have you?'

'Just temporary, Jacko. As temporary as I can make it.'

'Your dad's not there any more, of course . . .'

Wicksy muffled a sigh. Jacko wouldn't be content until he'd had a full update.

'I haven't seen him in a while. He's still around these parts, I think, but I haven't a clue where. Can't say I care much, either.'

'But of course Brian's not your real dad, is he? I remember Pat sayin' somethin' about that . . .'

'He's my stepdad,' Wicksy said, hoping it didn't sound too snappish. 'I haven't seen my real Dad, my Mum's first husband that is, since I was a nipper. He lives over in Walford. Name of Beale. Pete Beale.'

There, he thought. That's the lot, apart from blood groups.

'Families,' Jacko said. 'They're nothin' but trouble to a fella, right? I'm sure I'd have made a lot more of myself if my old man hadn't held me back. I mean, it's not as if they really help, is it? Not like they're cracked up to do.

9

You hear all these stories about men makin' it in the world an' it's all thanks to their mum or their dad. That's what you *hear*. But I don't know of anybody that was really helped along by their parents. More often than not a kid's just somethin' they take out their frustrations on. Take yourself as an example. You were lugged from one broken marriage into another one that broke up. No sense of security. You could have turned into a right bad lot an' it would have been down to your folks, right?'

'Yeah, I suppose so.'

'I'll tell you somethin', Simon. I know a bloke that was brought up in Dr Barnardo's an' he reckons it was the most secure-feelin' time of his life. Now that's somethin', isn't it? That makes you think.'

It made Wicksy think it was time to clear out of there, before Jacko got into his stride. Half a chance and he'd go into an hour-long monologue without stopping for breath.

'That's the bottlin' taken care of, Jacko. I best be goin'. Got lots to do.'

Jacko glanced at the filled shelves, surprised the job had been done so quickly.

'Fancy a swift half before you go?'

'Nah, thanks all the same.' Wicksy got his jacket. 'I don't like drinkin' durin' the day. Makes me sleepy.'

'Fair enough,' Jacko said. 'I reckon I'll have one myself. I could do with feelin' sleepy. That way, maybe I can kip the afternoon away. It gets a bit dreary bein' here on my own.' He walked to the door, shoulders stooped as he undid the bolts. 'See you tonight, then.'

Wicksy said he would be there at eight sharp. Going down the side of the pub to the main road he pictured Jacko sitting at a table in his empty pub with a light ale for company. He had an empty life, that man. Dozens of

10

customers, mostly regulars, but not one friend. Maybe it was no wonder, considering Jacko's nature and his boring chat, but all the same it was a shame. He wasn't a bad man. There must be somebody, somewhere, who would want to be his mate.

Wicksy got to the corner and stopped, wondering why he was so concerned for Jacko when his own circumstances were so bad, so much worse than the guv'nor's. What friends or consolations did Simon Wicks have? None he could think of. Jacko at least had his own business, a roof over his head and money in the bank. He had compensations in his life. He had security.

Security. Now there was something, a real goal if ever there was one. It hadn't concerned Wicksy a year ago. Or six months ago. But now . . .

He looked along the road and saw it coming, the dark green Toyota saloon.

'Shit!'

He turned sharply and walked back along the side of the pub, hoping they hadn't seen him. He would bet they were on the lookout for him. Nothing desperate. Not yet. Just making their presence felt, reminding him. One week. He had one short week. The date hung relentlessly in his mind and it had the power to make him feel sick. 7th October. Black Monday.

He waited by the corner door of the pub until he was sure the car would be gone, then went back to the main road. There were a lot of cars about, but the dark green one wasn't anywhere in sight. It wasn't exactly a relief, just a lessening of tension. Wicksy lived with tension. That would tell on him in his old age, he reckoned. If he ever got to old age.

'Simon Wicks Esquire.'

He had been so busy looking at cars he hadn't noticed

the people. This character was one he would have avoided with the same energy he'd used to avoid that Toyota. Wicksy tried to look nonchalant.

'Inspector Grace. How's it goin?'

'Same as ever, Simon. A lot of villainy about, as usual, so I'm a busy man.'

'Well . . .' Wicksy shrugged, disliking the way Grace was looking at him. 'It's good to be busy, I suppose.'

'Busy yourself, eh?'

'Not as much as I'd like to be. Part-time workin', that kind of thing.' He gave himself a mental kick. Part-time cash-in-hand work wasn't something you mentioned to a nosey copper. 'But I'm always on the lookout,' Wicksy hurried on. 'No sense givin' in, even if good jobs are scarce as hens' teeth.'

'Oh, I'm sure a sharp lad like you can make his way, whatever the obstacles.'

Inspector Grace was wide and fat. He had a florid, small-featured face that gave him the appearance of a large, corrupted infant. The corners of his mouth turned down like puffy commas. His voice was gravelly from too much smoking and his breath smelt stale and fishy. He was built for menace, entrenched tightly in the authority of his blue uniform.

'Haven't been getting into any more trouble that'd require my attention, have you?'

'I've never been in that kind of trouble,' Wicksy said, holding the policeman's gaze. 'You know that, Mr Grace.'

'No, I don't know that, Simon.'

'The business with the car was a misunderstanding.'

'I didn't misunderstand a thing about it, Simon. You were drunk and you were driving dangerously. You know it and I know it.'

'The magistrates said different.'

'Magistrates know piss-all about crafty, sweet-talking little villains that can worm their way out of anything, so long as there's enough sentimentality on hand to help them through.'

'You don't have the right to talk to me like that,' Wicksy said, wishing this was a civilian insulting him, so he could at least lay a decent threat on him. 'An' even though I don't need to, I'll remind you the breathalyser didn't show a thing, an' the so-called eye-witness report was trumped up by an old dear who didn't like me drivin' down her road after eleven at night.'

Grace's eyes had taken on a faraway look. 'Do you know what the word "insolent" means?' he said.

Wicksy was silent.

'Insolent, smart-arsed, mouthy – all much the same thing, and you're all of them, lad. I knew it the minute I laid eyes on you, and I was even surer when your foul-mouthed mummy weighed in on the defence side, between hiccups.' The Inspector leaned closer. 'I've got ways with the likes of you, sonny boy. Don't chance your arm. Know what I mean?'

Wicksy knew this character's reputation. He liked nerve games. He needled people: he had even managed to make a villain attack him once, just to get a conviction – *any* conviction. Things were bad enough for Wicksy right now without running foul of Inspector Grace; but there was his pride. His pride didn't budge for politics or discretion or anything else.

'Bollocks,' he said, closing the distance between their faces by another inch.

The Inspector's right arm twitched forward, stopped. His mouth churned for a second.

'If we weren't on a main street, Wicks – '

'You might stand a chance of gettin' your pills kicked,

13

fatso. A no-witness job. You'd hate that, wouldn't you?'

'Now listen – '

'*You* listen.' Wicksy's ears were singing. 'It's easy to be a hard man out in the open with the law backin' you. But one day the law won't be there. You must be due for hangin' up the old truncheon, yeah? Soon, anyway. That's the day you'll wish you'd learned a bit of decency an' charity. I reckon there's plenty of lads'll be in the queue that bright mornin', just dyin' to even things up a bit.'

This time Grace's arm came forward and didn't stop. He grabbed Wicksy's elbow. He tried to twist the arm but Wicksy kept it stiff.

'I can pull you in right now. I can lay any one of a dozen charges – your word against mine.'

'Go ahead an' try it,' Wicksy said, thinking fast. 'It might be your word against mine, but I reckon a bit of dirt'll stick when I tell them I wouldn't do the filthy obscene thing you asked me to do, an' that you pulled me in on a false charge because I wouldn't. Like you said – I can convince some people dead easy. Magistrates, judges for all I know.'

'You little bastard!'

'Yeah. I can be.'

Grace withdrew his hand. He looked about him to see if anybody had been watching. Then he looked at Wicksy, raising a finger.

'You better keep well clear of me in future. You're on my list, as of now.' The normally reddish flush on Grace's cheeks had shifted towards purple. 'One wrong move . . .'

'Is it all right if I go about my lawful business now?'

'Piss off!'

As casually as he could, given the state of his nerves, Wicksy walked off along the road.

There was no justice, he decided. Not if justice meant

14

what he thought it meant. If you did right by the world, didn't harm anybody, didn't go out of your way to cause pain or hardship – that kind of behaviour should entitle a bloke to decent treatment by other people, by life itself. But there was no justice. Life and other people were against him. They snarled, threatened, pried and connived. Nowhere was there a helping hand or a gesture of kindness. Not a solitary trace of warmth.

How was it possible to be so friendless? That really was a hell of a situation. Worse, he made enemies without trying. There was no one to console him, to offer peace or hope of a solution to his terrible problem.

The problem reared suddenly in his mind: *October 7th*. He glanced about him, trying not to let the blackness of it overwhelm him.

He forced his thoughts to Beckie. She should be a comfort to him and maybe in time she would be. But he didn't have much time. Right now, in spite of anything he told Jacko or anybody else, the relationship with the pretty Beckie was at a brittle, uncertain stage. There was nothing there Wicksy could rely on, let alone take comfort from.

October 7th.

'God . . .'

He stopped outside a café, looked through the window first to make sure there was no one there he didn't want to meet, then went in.

'Cup of frothy, love,' he said to the overalled girl behind the counter. 'An' a jam doughnut.'

He always fancied something sweet when he was worried. Since he was worried most of the time now he was putting his teeth and his weight in a lot of jeopardy, but the craving was something he couldn't help. Sugary things soothed him.

He was halfway through the doughnut when he looked up and realized he should have done one other thing when he looked through the window: he should have checked to see if there was a back door. Which there wasn't. Standing in the doorway was Brian Wicks, his stepfather, looking round the place with his proprietorial eyes. For a man who owned and controlled practically nothing, Brian always gave the impression he was a wheel.

He saw Wicksy, nodded, made his order at the counter then came over and sat opposite.

'Where have you been hidin' yourself, then?' he said. 'Must be six months since I've seen you around.'

'I thought maybe you'd be the one that was in hidin',' Wicksy said, not really wanting a barney but unable, as usual, to be civil to Brian. 'After that business with the Waterford crystal so-called seconds . . .'

'Leave it out,' Brian said. 'I was took in by the geezer that flogged me the stuff.'

'You should have done your homework. Waterford never have seconds. They smash them all up. You were floggin' perfect goods. Knocked-off goblets an' vases at knock-down prices.' Wicksy grinned. 'A few people got a bargain out of you before the law showed up an' you had to do a runner.'

'That's all blown over,' Brian said, tight-jawed. 'They never connected any of it with me.' He glanced over his shoulder, as he often did. 'Seen your mum lately, at all?'

'I'm stoppin' with her at the moment.'

'Same place? Dover Road?'

Wicksy nodded.

'I might slip round an' see her some time.'

'What would you want to do that for?'

Brian glared. There were times when the easy-flaring

16

violence in him was like a light shining at the back of his eyes.

'I've a right to see Pat any time I like. I don't have to make excuses.'

'But I wondered why.' It was never a good idea to put Brian's back up, but it was never an easy thing for Wicksy to avoid, either. 'Last time you saw her, I'm told, you were pretty heavy with the threats. I can't remember you ever bein' nice to her. Why don't you just leave her alone an' let her get on with her life?'

'An' why don't you keep your beak out of what doesn't concern you?' It was a sharp instruction, not a question or a suggestion. 'That's always been your trouble, Simon.' Brian tapped his own nose. 'Too much of this. Even when you were a little kid.'

'Natural curiosity, that's what it is. I probably got it from my dad.'

Brian's eyes narrowed. 'You like needlin' me, don't you?'

'Well.' Wicksy shrugged. 'Maybe you just keep comin' across me on bad days. My needlin' days. Seems I've been doin' a bit more than usual this afternoon.'

'Ah well, what the hell,' Brian said, surprisingly. 'Maybe we're both just a bit edgy, eh?'

Wicksy wondered what he was up to. Brian wasn't a man to back down or make peace so easily. He enjoyed getting a row going, once it was started.

'I'm glad I bumped into you like this, Simon.' The tone had become confidential. 'One thing you've always had is a good business head. I could use a bit of advice.'

This was news to Wicksy. Since when had he possessed a head for business?

'I need to organize somethin',' Brian went on. 'It's a big scheme, biggest I've handled, an' if I get it right it'll

17

be the makin' of me.' He winked. 'I'm always one to show the right kind of gratitude to the ones that's helped me. Give me a bit of a leg up here, Simon, an' I don't think you'll find yourself regrettin' it.'

'How can I help you?'

'Like I said, on the organizin' side.'

Wicksy was trying to figure out if he could trust the glimmer of hope he felt. Was Brian offering him a chance to make a quick buck? Quick enough to get him out of the hole he was in?

'It's statuettes,' Brian said, his thin mouth curving in a smile.

'Statuettes?'

'That's right. Little ones, head an' shoulder jobs, for sittin' on desks an' sideboards an' bookshelves an' all that. Made out of plaster an' painted in different colours.'

'But who are they? Shakespeare, stuff like that?'

'Nah. Pop stars. All the latest crowd – about twenty different ones for starters, but there'll be plenty more, an' we'd never run out of a market, would we? Not the way the fashions in pop keep changin'.'

'You mean you're talkin' about *manufacturin*' the things?'

'That's right. I'm talkin' about handlin' the design, manufacture, packagin', the lot.'

Wicksy was staring. Brian had never been known to tackle anything adequately in the area of street-corner and back-door sales. How could he hope to handle a project like this? Maybe his mind had snapped. He'd never struck Wicksy as being mentally robust.

'How do you get started? It's a bit ambitious. You've got to get all the gear together, then find somebody that can use it – then there's distribution. That's a whole ball game in itself.'

18

'Sure, sure.' Brian waved his hand casually, dismissing the possibility of snags. 'Look, let me fill you in. First, I stumbled on this goldmine. A bloke. Little old fella, a wizard with his hands. For years an' years he's been makin' these statuettes of people he knows an' people in the news an' film stars an' such. It's a hobby with him. I was in the Drake's Drum one night an' he showed one he'd done of the guv'nor. Talk about lifelike. The man's a genius, nothin' short of. But he's never turned this talent of his into cash. I told him he should, an' he said he'd like to, but he'd no idea how to get started. So I went away for a couple of days, thought about it a lot, then put a proposition to him. He makes the statuettes, I handle the business of turnin' them into money, an' he gets a cut.'

'What kind of cut?'

'Ten percent.'

'You always were the generous one.'

Brian looked hurt. 'It's me that's got to supply the plaster, the mouldin' rubber, the paint, the packagin'. That'll cost. All he does is whittle a bit of wood, make a mould out of it, then pour in the plaster an' dip the finished articles in paint. He can sit on his bum all day doin' that while I'm buzzin' round like a blue-arsed fly doin' the business. Fair's fair, Simon.'

'What about copyright?'

'What about it?'

'Well it's obvious, isn't it? You can't just cash in on umpteen people's fame without payin' them a cut, can you? It's against the law.'

Brian spread his hands. 'That's a small problem we'll sort out when we come to it.'

Wicksy shook his head slowly. 'They'll put you away if you don't get it sorted out right at the start.'

'So I'll take advice on the matter, OK? See, there's my very point, Simon. Your business head. You spotted that snag straight away. Sharp thinkin'.'

'So how else do you think I can help you? What is it you actually want me to do?'

Brian looked over his shoulder for a second. 'I need a bit of assistance on the organizin' side, like I already said. You know, settin' the scheme up.'

Wicksy could imagine himself doing something like Brian proposed, and doing it quite well. He couldn't see Brian running the show, though. He hadn't the straight-line thinking or the staying power to finish the Mirror crossword. The big question, though, was whether there was an immediate and sizable sub available, something to throw into the teeth of October 7th.

'I can't handle all the organizin' myself,' Brian said. 'That's obvious. It needs a bit of clout to get things goin', right?'

Wicksy nodded.

'So, I was thinkin', if you could let me have fifty, say, just to get it off the ground . . .'

'Fifty what?' Wicksy said, his heart dropping.

'What do you think? Fifty quid. Just to help out with gettin' the first batches of material an' a few boxes. Short term loan, to be paid back with a handsome bit of interest when we're in production.'

'I should have known. You're not after my business head. You're wantin' permission to put your hand in my hip pocket.'

Brian looked huffy. 'I wouldn't have put it that way myself, Simon. I was approachin' the matter in business-like terms. This would be called initial investment, wouldn't it? With the promise of rapid growth on capital input.'

'The pocket's empty,' Wicksy said. 'Where do you think I'd get fifty quid I could sling about? Or twenty, for that matter?'

'I thought you'd be rollin' in it by now.'

That showed how much Brian knew about anything. He couldn't even use his eyes. In a dozen little ways, Wicksy knew he had the *look* of a young man down on his luck.

'The last time I talked to you,' Brian said, 'the last time we had a real talk that is, was about a year ago. You told me – '

'It wasn't a talk,' Wicksy interrupted. 'It was a slanging match, nearly from the word go.'

Brian nodded, his eyes hard again. 'Yeah, I slagged you off, all right. Because of your mouth. All that braggin' you were doin' about your band, an' how you were goin' to make it big with gigs right an' left an' a recordin' contract an' God knows what else in the pipeline. What happened to all that? I mean, I could work it out for myself, you didn't make it as big as you reckoned you would, but with all that confidence and the talent you said you had an' the work that was lined up, I'd have expected you to be makin' a decent livin' out of music by now.'

'It didn't work out,' Wicksy said.

'Christ. After all that chat.'

'Yeah, well. There were problems. A personality clash here an' there, a few gigs that got cancelled, things like that. The band broke up a while ago.'

Brian was exuding disdain. 'So you've not even got a job?'

'No. Not a real one. Have you?'

'What's that supposed to mean?'

'I might be in the crap right now,' Wicksy said, 'But by

21

the time I'm your age, I'm pretty sure I'll be set up. That's what I meant.'

Before Brian could say any more or his anger could get a chance to take hold of him, Wicksy stood up and pushed back his chair.

'I'll see you around,' he said.

Brian muttered something at the table top.

Out on the street again Wicksy wondered if he should go back to his mother's place. Going there wasn't a natural thing to do, he always had to make a decision about it. Other blokes he knew, people his own age, would finish work for the day and they would go home. It was natural. But Wicksy had no sense of home. Where was home? Not his mother's gaff. Not anywhere. That was one item he had left off the list of gloom – he was a man without a home.

At least, though, his mother's place was sanctuary. Putting up with her moaning and her drinking bouts was nothing, not if he considered the alternative. In the house at Dover Road he would at least be safe. Nowadays Wicksy felt eyes jabbing his back when he walked the streets. It wasn't possible to be easygoing any more.

There was no sign of Pat when he got to the house. In the kitchen he found a note.

Met Sid and Angelo.
Gone to a party.

A party. Not even five o'clock yet and she had gone to a party. That was big frowzy Pat all over. Wicksy sometimes thought he hated her. Other times he believed he was just indifferent to her. He never felt like he was her son, or that she bestowed anything maternal on him. That was one more for the list – he was a man without a mother.

But he did have a father. He only remembered Pete Beale vaguely, a big smiling man, a man with strong hands and a kind face. Wicksy stood by the window, wondering. Could his dad, his real dad, get him out of the trouble he was in?

He turned away sharply. That was useless daydreaming. His father hadn't laid eyes on him in donkey's years. He wouldn't even recognize him. They had nothing in common, and Wicksy suspected it took more than the bare ties of blood to make one man stand up for another.

There was a knock at the door.

Wicksy went to the hall and stopped. It couldn't be them, he told himself. They didn't know where he lived any more. When they'd asked where he had moved to he told them something vague about dossing down temporarily at one or two mates' places. Even so, they were crafty. How could he be sure that wasn't them out there?

The letter box was pushed open. Wicksy dodged back into the lounge.

'Pat?' a woman's voice squeaked. 'You in there, Pat?'

Wicksy groaned, partly with relief. He went into the hall and opened the door. Joyce Midgeley was on the step wearing her usual over-bright expression. Her mascara was thicker than usual today, but it still failed to distract attention from the sag lines under her eyes. The lipstick, Wicksy thought, made her mouth resemble two little segments of an orange.

'Mum's not in. She's at a party somewhere with Sid and Angelo.'

'Oh dear.' The wide-eyed brightness dimmed. 'I was sure she told me she'd be in this afternoon.'

'She probably did,' Wicksy said. 'You know Mum. Long-term plans don't hold up with her. She's a spur-of-the-moment woman – especially where whoopin' it up's concerned.'

'I brought a bottle, an' all.' Joyce pulled a brown paper bag from her raincoat pocket. 'I was really lookin' forward to havin' a natter with Pat. We've not done that for ages.'

Three weeks at least, Wicksy thought. Joyce and his mother were old companions who reminisced in circles, always talking about their heyday which sounded, from the snippets Wicksy had picked up, like a really horrendous period in their lives. Drink and illicit sex were the main topics they giggled over, and those wild days had certainly left their marks on the pair of them.

'Why don't you bring your bottle in an' I'll drink with you to the top of the label,' Wicksy said, aware that in spite of everything, he had some sympathy for Joyce. Maybe it was pity. 'You never know, Mum might get fed up with her party an' turn up while you're here.'

'Ooh, what a good idea. Thanks, Si. You're a good boy.'

'Of course I am.'

Wicksy stepped back and let Joyce in. As he followed her along the hall he couldn't help smiling. A year ago he had pictured himself living in a Mayfair pad by now, entertaining glossy upmarket dollies with champagne and caviar. Who'd have guessed he would wind up like this, hiding out from loan sharks in his mother's council house and sharing a bottle of cheap gin with a poor old cow like Joyce Midgeley?

Wednesday

The setting and interior of the Duke's Head rendered the place anonymous. No casual visitor to the pub could ever describe it afterwards except in vague terms – it was at the end of a run-down street; inside was a long bar curved at one end, a few tables, a brownish carpet, some brass on the walls and a permanently smoky atmosphere. The beer, all of it keg, was as characterless as the premises. On the other hand strangers did tend to recall, clearly, the barmaid who worked there four days and five evenings a week. She was in her forties, sturdily built, with geometrically styled blonde hair, a hard, once-pretty face and a manner that oscillated between brash over-friendliness at one end of the scale and ferocious hostility at the other. In between she could demonstrate coyness, gross sexual insinuation, conspiracy and a talent for gossip that kept regulars from mentioning anything confidential within twenty feet of the woman.

She was Pat Harris, once Pat Wicks, and on that wet morning, six days from her son's Armageddon, he sat at a corner table in the Duke's Head watching his mother perform and wondering, in a depressed way, what he had ever done to deserve her.

'Duggie was sayin' how he prefers women with thin legs,' Pat was telling her friend, Steph, who was perched on a stool halfway along the bar. 'Then he gets in an argument with old Roger, who says he likes plump legs better. So I cuts in an' tells them I prefer somethin' between the two.'

Steph let out a rasping laugh as Pat turned away to serve another customer. In his corner Wicksy looked at his glass of Coke and sighed. He was sure Pat didn't realize what her style did for her reputation. Even people who lacked the evidence that she was a loose-living slut developed the certainty within minutes of listening to her. Pat was the leading figure in numerous dirty jokes, she figured in countless grubby legends about the late sixties and the seventies, and more than one marriage had collapsed because of her. All that, Wicksy thought, and so much more, yet he knew there was a wounded, hurting woman at the centre of Pat. All her outward behaviour denied such a thing, but Wicksy knew nevertheless. Pat's denial was so fierce and relentless that to Wicksy the wounded part of her seemed like another woman. She was the one he could pity.

'What do you reckon to this?' a punter asked Pat, fingering the three-day stubble on his chin.

'Terrible,' Pat snapped. He was one she didn't like. 'You look ridiculous, know that?'

'I reckon it'll look good in a week or so.'

'An' I reckon you should shave it off now an' save yourself all the embarrassment.'

The landlord, Duggie, was fixing a fresh bottle of whisky to an optic. As he began hooking it up on the gantry Pat turned and tickled his armpits. He let out a roar and leapt away from her. The bottle hurtled to the floor. It landed with a bump but didn't break. There was laughter and applause from the punters standing at the bar.

'Bloody hell, Pat!' Duggie snatched up the whisky and put it on the shelf. 'That was a stupid thing to do!'

Pat scowled at him. 'What's up with you? Can't you take a joke no more?'

'That bottle could have smashed!'

'But it didn't, did it?'

'That's not the point!'

Pat turned and addressed the customers. 'You'll have to forgive old sourpuss,' she said. 'He hasn't been gettin' any lately an' it's makin' him grumpy.'

More laughter and Duggie stamped off through to the back, his face crimson.

'I don't know how you keep your job,' Steph said, 'what with the things you say to him an' the liberties you take.'

Pat winked. 'He fancies me. Can't you tell?'

'Can't say I'd noticed, no.'

'Oh yeah. Always lustin' after me, that one. I have to put stuff in his tea for his own good. I mean, it got so bad he tripped on a loose board back here one day an' pole-vaulted into the cellar.'

Amid renewed laughter there was a sharp rap on the end of the bar. Pat saw a stranger standing there, frowning at her. He was in his forties, tall and well-dressed, with the kind of face that had authority built in.

'What can I do for you, darlin'?' Pat said, approaching him.

'I'd like a drink, if it's not too much trouble.'

'No trouble at all,' Pat said, her voice tightening. 'What would you like?'

'A brandy.'

'A brandy it is.'

Pat turned to the shelf of glasses behind the bar, throwing a sour look at Steph. As she reached out for a shot glass the man called out to her.

'In a *brandy* glass, if you please.'

'These are what we put brandy in,' Pat said, holding up the shot glass.

27

The man's frown deepened. 'Are you saying you don't have proper brandy glasses?'

'I'm sayin' this is what we put brandy in.'

'I see. Tell the landlord I want to speak to him, will you?'

'I'm not sure if he's available,' Pat snapped, putting on her stubborn face.

'I saw your antics with him a minute ago,' the man said stiffly. 'I'm sure he can't be far away. Fetch him, will you?'

Something unusual in the customer's self-assurance made Pat hold back from telling him to sling his hook. She went through to the back where Duggie, a thin and asthmatic man, was struggling to stack crates of empty bottles by the rear door.

'There's some toffee-nosed git at the bar wants to talk to you.'

'Oh, gawd . . .' Duggie put down the crate he was holding. 'Isn't it somethin' you can deal with?'

'No. He insists on seein' you.'

Duggie shuffled out to the bar behind Pat. She pointed to where the tall man was standing. Duggie went forward, head tilted enquiringly.

'I've just been told by your barmaid that you don't serve brandy in the correct kind of glass,' the man said.

'We serve it in these,' Duggie said, pointing to the rows of shot glasses.

'I know. You shouldn't.'

'Cheeky bugger,' Pat murmured.

The man glared at her. 'Did you say something?'

'Maybe I did, maybe I didn't.'

'I think we'll come back to that.' The man looked at Duggie again. 'At the rear of the premises, or somewhere else where you and your staff can clearly see it, there

28

should be a poster with a large heading over it which says "Get the Glass Right". Underneath there are outline drawings of all the glasses you should use, and alongside each there's a list of the drinks appropriate to the particular glass. Now tell me, do you have that poster on display in this pub?'

'What's it to you?' Pat demanded.

'Do you have it on display?' the man repeated, ignoring Pat.

'Well . . .' Duggie was frowning. 'I know I saw it, I mean I looked at it when it came in, but . . .' He sighed. 'From the brewery, are you?'

'Yes,' the man said, 'you could say I'm from the brewery. My name is Lester and I'm a director of the brewery, in fact. I had business in Ilford today and I'd already noted we have three pubs in the area. So I thought I'd visit them. This place is the first on my list, and frankly I'm beginning to have discouraging feelings about calling at the other two.'

'Well, about the poster,' Duggie said uncomfortably, 'It was one of those things, it got overlooked because I'd a busy day or somethin' like that . . .'

'See that it gets tacked up as soon as possible. Make sure there are brandy glasses on the shelf, too. You *do* have a stock of them, don't you?'

'Um, yes I do. But they get broke so easily, them bein' so thin . . .'

'It's brewery policy that drinks in our licensed houses should always be served in the correct glasses – no matter how fragile they might be. Now.' Mr Lester switched his attention to Pat. 'Another point of company policy is that bar staff be polite and helpful to customers. You appear to be neither.'

'Depends on the customer,' Pat said huffily.

29

'They should all be treated alike,' Lester said firmly. 'I can't imagine what reason there could have been for hiring someone with your surly and impudent nature, when there are so many more suitable people crying out for jobs. However . . .' He turned to Duggie again. 'I'm not here to wield axes on behalf of the brewery. The general record of this house is good. I'll leave it to you to make whatever adjustments may be necessary to maintain the pub's good name.'

Duggie nodded gratefully. 'I'll go an' get you a glass for your brandy . . .'

'Don't bother,' Lester said. 'I've gone off the notion of a drink.'

Duggie and Pat stood and watched as he walked out.

'Right,' Duggie said through clenched teeth, 'a word through the back, Pat.'

In the far corner Wicksy watched, together with the other customers, as landlord and barmaid went through to the back room. They were gone for nearly a minute, then Pat came out, red in the neck. She walked to the end of the bar, snatched up her cigarettes and lighter from the back fitting, then went round the end of the bar and sat down at a table. Duggie, looking as flushed as Pat, started serving. Wicksy got up and took his glass across to where his mother was sitting.

'I thought you'd cleared off,' Pat said as he sat down.

'I was keepin' my usual low profile. What's this, anyway? Token strike or somethin'?'

'My five-minute break.' Pat lit a cigarette. 'I'd like to give that one over there a break. His leg, maybe, or his bloody neck.'

'You can't go blamin' Duggie.'

'Flamin' cheek he's got,' Pat went on, as if she hadn't heard Wicksy. 'Tellin' *me* I'm a threat to his trade. Jesus.

30

I'm the only reason half the punters come in here.'

'You made a right hash of handlin' that geezer from the brewery though, didn't you? Talk about winnin' friends an' influencin' people. I could see a mile off he was one of the kind you need to handle carefully.'

'Is that so, Mr Expert?'

'I've not worked in this trade as long as you, Mum,' Wicksy said, 'but I can spot the obvious a lot better than you. You've got no talent for handlin' people.'

'An' I suppose you have?' Pat blew a plume of smoke above Wicksy's head. 'That's why you're makin' such a success of your life, is it?'

'I started with one big disadvantage other blokes didn't have to put up with.'

'Watch it, Simon. You're not so big an' grown-up I wouldn't belt you one.'

Wicksy shook his head at his empty glass. 'Threats. What would my day be without a dose of threats.'

Pat examined his face. 'What's that mean?' she demanded.

'It means I'm permanently dodgin' flyin' muck. An' there's no sign of things gettin' any better. Just the opposite, in fact.'

Pat was no good at being motherly towards Wicksy and nowadays she never tried. Instead, whenever she felt it was necessary, she adopted the older-and-wiser role, doling out hard-headed advice untinged by maternal consolation or protectiveness.

'Your trouble is you've got champagne ambitions an' only beery talent. You get yourself into high-flyin' schemes without realizin' you're not the lad for the job. Stick at your own level an' you'll get on a lot better. You'll certainly get yourself in less trouble.'

31

'Fine advice for the future,' Wicksy said. 'But what do I do about the here-an'-now?'

'Do what I always did,' Pat said.

'An' what's that?'

'Use your wits an' don't rely on other people's help. They always let you down.'

For just a second Wicksy wished she was a real mother, for he had an overwhelming need to put his head on somebody's shoulder and admit how scared he was.

'I don't know what good my wits are goin' to be against a couple of gorillas that get their kicks makin' jigsaws out of people.'

'There's always an answer,' Pat said flatly.

'Yeah. An' I reckon I know what it's goin' to be in my case. A couple of weeks in intensive care, then learn to walk with a stick an' I'll be right as rain.'

'You're blowin' things up out of all proportion, Simon.'

He didn't believe he was. Pat didn't know the whole story. If he had told her she'd have ranted at him and that would only have added to his misery. All she knew was that he owed back payments on some musical instruments. The whole truth was more complex and a lot less humdrum. Wicksy believed, without a trace of doubt, that he was in danger of being comprehensively mutilated. And soon.

'I've got to do somethin',' he said. 'I can't just stand still an' let things happen to me. It's knowin' what to do, though.'

'Why don't you flog the car?'

'I've told you before. If I keep nothin' else, I'm keepin' my car.'

'You treat that banger like a lucky charm,' Pat said. 'It hasn't brought you much luck so far. For all you know it might be an *un*lucky charm. Gettin' rid of it might be the one thing that'd save your bacon.'

That was something else Pat didn't understand. His little yellow Spitfire was the last trace of any kind of style he possessed. Age didn't count with a car like that. Wicksy had stretched himself thin to get that beauty, and he would never let anybody take it away from him.

'I better go,' he said, standing up. 'I'm due at the Ginger Giant at half-twelve. Jacko's got a thing about punctuality.'

'Yeah,' Pat nodded. 'He's not bad to work for, though. I wouldn't mind bein' back there, instead of here.'

'You can't do that though, can you? You blew it. Just like you'll blow it in this place, if you carry on the way you did just now.'

'Thanks for the advice.'

'And thanks for yours, Mumsy,' Wicksy said as he walked away.

In the beginning it had been simple. They were a band – Eddie, Dave, Pete, Harry and Wicksy. They had individual talents that blended into sounds which were original without ever going offbeat. At small gigs and doing warm-ups at concerts they began to attract a solid following. Like all small units that showed promise, they had wanted to expand. To get the bigger gigs and the decent money they could certainly command, they needed to upgrade their image, which meant, mainly, improving their equipment. Wicksy, who was keyboards man, lyric writer and general fixer, took on the task of costing the upgrade. By cutting as many corners as he could without prejudicing quality, he came up with a figure of £1700. Between them they could afford just under £200 in hard cash.

Gloom set in. Harry, who was interested in exploring

what he called 'purer' musical forms, said they should forget the idea of getting bigger and flashier and concentrate on being unique. The others saw that, half-heartedly, as a definite alternative to expansion. But Wicksy wouldn't buy it. They needed £1500 to achieve their original ambition. So what was the big deal? Hire purchase was out, of course; they didn't have the credentials to satisfy the terms of any HP contract. But this was less than two grand they were talking about. How many good gigs would it take to raise that amount? Not many. In terms of current showbiz finances it was chickenfeed.

'So if it's chickenfeed,' Harry had said, 'let's see you come up with it.'

Wicksy said he would. Then he really began to wonder how he would fulfil such a promise. He studied advertisements for quick cash loans. As far as he could see, he had to be a property owner before he stood a chance of being considered. But he tried anyway, and was turned down flat by the three companies he approached. So he went to see a bank manager to discuss the possibility of the bank investing a trifling sum in the group's advancement. The manager listened, asked a few questions, then told Wicksy the bank would need no time to consider the proposition; he could have his answer right there and then, and the answer was no. Before Wicksy left, the manager assured him he would be wasting his time if he tried any other bank.

Still Wicksy wasn't deterred. The dream was too powerful, it wouldn't allow him to accept defeat. Success, the full-time pleasure of being a musician and living the glittering life of the pop star, lay beyond a single hurdle. He talked to Billy Edwards, a chap he had gone to school with who now did an unspecified job for a bookie. Wicksy explained his dilemma and asked Billy if he knew of any way a bloke could lay hands on a quick grand-and-a-half without having to leave an arm as security. Billy was generous and unhesitating with the information Wicksy needed. For a trouble-free loan, all he had to do was go to a loan firm – not the ones who advertised, though. The other kind. Their representatives could be found in various places and they never actually operated from an office address. If Wicksy wanted, Billy could put him in touch.

Excited as he was, Wicksy was sure there had to be a snag. Sure there was, Billy said. The interest rates were high. Very high. Swift repayment of the loan was the only way to reduce the pain of tough percentages. That was all right, Wicksy thought. They would pay back as fast as they could, leaving themselves clear and free to pile up their personal profits.

There was one other snag, Billy warned. People who fell behind with their payments were treated harshly. The interest could get staggeringly out of proportion, too, adding to the discomfort of the situation. Anyone who actually tried to welch on the loan, or fell too far behind with payments, could wind up with dodgy kneecaps. At least. And they would *still* owe the money.

That was grim news, but Wicksy saw no cause to worry over it. The loan would be a short-term, straight-up transaction from the band's point of view. Their involvement with the loan sharks would be brief, no complications. Wicksy thanked Billy Edwards for his help and asked him to arrange an introduction with one of the money men the following day.

That night he told the band what he had lined up. With the possible exception of Harry, they were delighted. They agreed to a five-way cut from their income to meet

35

the loan repayments and were happy to let Wicksy attend to the details.

In a betting shop next day he was introduced to a severe-looking, fleshy man with a deep scar on his nose. He was called Sid Benson. He looked at Wicksy the way a doctor would examine an infection: his eyes probed, measured, diagnosed. Wicksy explained how much he wanted and what he wanted it for. Benson nodded. He told Wicksy about the straightforward repayment system, how the collections were made, and the consequences of anyone falling behind or being silly enough to think they could run out on the deal. After Wicksy had given his address – at that time he was sharing a flat with one of the band – and had been assured that he'd be checked out discreetly and swiftly, he left the betting shop with the promise that Benson would see him at the same place and time tomorrow.

It had all been so simple. The money was in Wicksy's hands twenty-four hours after he had asked for it. He told himself that if a man hung on to his dream, there was nothing he couldn't achieve. He gave no thought to the possibility that the dream could melt and give way to nightmare.

'How did you lot come to split up, anyway?' Beckie asked him that Wednesday night as they drove to a pub they both liked to use midweek. 'You always gave the impression you were inseparable.'

'You mean you noticed me back then? You knew who I was?'

'Sure. I'd got you weighed up more than a year ago.'

'Well, well . . .'

It was dark outside but in the slanting flashes of lamplight Wicksy could see Beckie clearly. She was small and compact, an eighteen-year-old who looked about

36

twenty with make-up, sixteen without it. Tonight she was made-up, of course: fine blonde eyebrows skilfully darkened, cheeks smoothed pale almond with a touch of peachy blusher, small mouth light pink and glossed. The colour of her hair defied classification. Beckie called it hi-tech blonde, which was to say it had a lot of blonde in it, with several shades of brown and traces of antique gold. Overall Beckie was a prize and Wicksy knew it. He also knew she didn't quite fit with him, because of a wide difference in their personalities, but the effect was good. He liked being seen with her and she was fond of letting other girls see she went around with one of the best looking lads in Ilford. Effect, for the time being, was all their relationship was about; neither seemed ready to take the other very seriously.

'I always thought you were a bit flash,' Beckie said as the car pulled into the yard outside the pub. 'The whole lot of you, I mean. You seemed to have just a bit too much confidence.'

'Oh, we had plenty of it, that's for sure.'

Wicksy stopped the car and switched off the engine. He turned and looked at Beckie. Now, in the light from the porchway of the pub, her hair looked dark, with highlighted filaments of gold.

'To answer your question, Beckie, we broke up because things didn't balance out. What we wanted an' what we got were very different. And what we were able to do was a lot less than we thought we could.'

'All that confidence – there was nothing to back it?'

'I wouldn't say that. But we discovered we couldn't hold together after a while. That was because we were edging into a bigger league, an' frankly I don't think we belonged there. Small was beautiful, we just didn't believe it at the time.'

'Will you get another band together some day?' Beckie asked.

He believed he would, if he ever survived to make the effort. For the moment he didn't want to think or talk about the future. That was bound to be bad luck and he was already cornering the market in that commodity.

'We'd better get inside,' he said, opening his door. 'You know how packed it gets after nine.'

The place was called Mickey's, after the owner who had bought it as a run-down pub and had worked hard to turn its fortunes round by attracting the young crowd. That had happened, in spite of the complaints of locals who had seen their favourite old drinking hole transformed into a spangly cocktail palace with piped music and a clientele who made a lot of noise on the streets after closing time. As no more than an act of protest – it had to be that, since they obviously didn't enjoy themselves – a knot of older people, men in their fifties and sixties, nightly colonized one end of the purple-painted bar, talking and drinking amongst themselves and steadfastly refusing to let anyone shift them.

It was one of these men who turned as Beckie walked in ahead of Wicksy. He looked from her pretty face to her prominently filled tee shirt, her tight jeans and knee boots, then he looked all the way up again, more slowly. He muttered something to the man beside him, who put a hand over his mouth, elaborately smothering a laugh. Wicksy hadn't failed to notice. He stepped across to the man, who was suddenly pretending he was on another planet.

'Excuse me.' Wicksy tapped the man's shoulder. 'I believe you made some comment about the young lady who's with me.'

38

'Eh?' The man blinked at Wicksy. 'What're you talkin' about?'

'You know what. Now I'd like you to apologize.'

The man blinked again, like a camera shutter slicing an instant of time. What he saw was what a number of people had seen, but only if they had asked for it, because it was an attitude, a forcefulness and promise of aggression that Wicksy would never have revealed without provocation. The smiling, easygoing youth had departed for the moment. In his place was a hard-eyed lad who could handle himself. He required an apology as an alternative to demonstrating just what he could do – and he wouldn't back down.

'Push off, sonny,' the man said, obviously feeling safe enough among his mates.

'Listen, you dirty-mouthed old git, I want an apology before I move off this spot.' Wicksy glanced aside for an instant. Beckie was standing a couple of yards away, tapping her foot as she stared at the young people laughing and drinking along the length of the bar. 'Now just tell the lady you're sorry an' you can get back to your pint.'

'An' what happens if I don't apologize?'

'I'll ruin your evenin'.'

The man tried to sneer, but he hadn't the necessary indifference to Wicksy's threat. Imperceptibly the other members of the group had detached themselves from his growing predicament. He tried squaring up to Wicksy.

'You know I could give you a good kickin', don't you?'

'Yeah, I know,' Wicksy said. 'If I lay down an' let you get on with it. But I'm not likely to do that.'

For three beats they stared at each other, the man's eyes desperately trying to match the firmness of Wicksy's.

Then the tense line broke as the man looked down for a second.

'What the hell,' he muttered. 'Anythin' for a quiet life.'

He walked across to Beckie, muttered something to her, then went back to the bar without looking at Wicksy.

'Cheers, Galahad,' Beckie said as Wicksy steered her to a stool near the far end. 'It wasn't really necessary, you know.'

'What? Gettin' him to apologize?'

'No. Showing me what a hard number you are. I'm not turned on by stuff like that. Maybe you are, of course.'

Wicksy realized she was annoyed. He clambered on to the stool next to her and ordered the drinks – white wine and soda water for Beckie, a lager for himself. Then he sat drumming his fingers, feeling his own annoyance begin to boil. All he had done was treat her like a lady, after all. And show her she wasn't here with a lout. A secondary annoyance was that voice of hers. Not posh exactly, but a shade further up market than those he was used to. She seemed to put it on stronger when she was upset about anything. Wicksy turned to her.

'I'm sorry,' he said. He wasn't, but he didn't want any bitching. He wanted to forget his worries for a couple of hours. 'I suppose I should have let it pass. Sorry, sorry.'

Beckie shrugged. 'Forget it,' she said.

Wicksy took a few swift gulps of lager, trying to melt the hard edges of sobriety. He always felt easier with Beckie when he wasn't entirely sober.

'If you ever do get a band up again, will you try to make a living at it?'

Wicksy hadn't expected her to speak first. He'd had the feeling there would need to be a small thawing, initiated by himself.

'Everybody hopes they can make a living at it,' he said.

'But next time I'd be more realistic than I was before. You have to get yourself organized. More rules, more stickin' to them, more rehearsals instead of sittin' around talkin' about the music scene and havin' fantasies out loud about how great it'll be when we hit the big time. An' a proper agent an' accountant lookin' after us.'

'They're all the things you didn't do last time?'

'Them an' a lot more.'

The list was endless, mostly small things that had finally splintered the band. Harry's constant agitation, his accusations that Wicksy's music was a cheap sell-out; the arguments, the new-flowering jealousies; the gigs that didn't materialize, the rip-offs on the fees. The list went on and on; each day there seemed to be new ground for dissent and disorder. Then a day came when there was no band, and all Wicksy was left with was the debt. That terrible debt. It was all down to him, nobody else wanted to know. He felt himself shuddering now and hoped it didn't show.

'I used to go out with a boy who was in a professional band,' Beckie said. 'He was all anarchy and freedom up on stage – you know, that wild thing in a good musician that convinces you he couldn't be tamed by anybody or anything. But he was a professional, and in real life he was *very* organized. Rehearsed regularly, had an agent and a manager, had nothing to do with drugs, drank very little and got to bed early. It really surprised me.'

'What made you move from professionals to failed amateurs?'

Wicksy asked the question coldly. He didn't want to hear about her past conquests, even if the story happened to confirm that his ideas about organization went along the right lines.

41

'It's people I go for, Simon, not their jobs. I've never been a groupie.'

'Sorry,' he said again. 'I suppose I'm bein' too touchy tonight. I don't know what's doin' it.'

'It's not only been tonight,' Beckie said. 'You've been moody and touchy by turns lately. Sometimes you're better at covering it than others.'

The night was going to take a big nosedive. Wicksy knew it and he didn't know any way to stop it happening. He hadn't the zing to keep a girl entertained and diverted, and worse than that he was past being able to fake it. He should have stayed in his mother's house and saved the few pounds he couldn't afford to spend making himself and Beckie miserable.

'Is something worrying you?'

'Nothin' in particular.' Wicksy wondered if it would be better to level with Beckie. That way, at least, she would understand why he was so low. It could also be the way to guarantee her exit from his life. 'Lately I've been tryin' to make solid plans for my future. That can be depressin'. Opportunities aren't what they were.'

'I suppose not.'

Beckie, he could see, was trying to be interested, but she was struggling against the natural impulse to enjoy herself in an atmosphere designed precisely for that. Her boot was tapping the spar of the stool in time to the music from the wall speakers and she looked about her as she spoke. The last thing she needed was a hard-times tale. She needed laughs. Wicksy struggled to brighten himself.

'There's Linda over there,' Beckie said, pointing to a girl standing near the pool table with her arm on a young man's shoulder. 'You remember her, don't you? I introduced you once.'

'Yeah. I remember her.'

'Should we go over and say hello? Linda's good fun.'

Beckie was already halfway off her stool, even though Wicksy didn't want to talk to the brittle little Linda, who annoyed him with her twittering and her shrill giggles and her constant sexual innuendo. Linda was a drag, and tonight Wicksy knew he would find her draggier than usual. But for peace, and to keep his relationship with Beckie as close to stability as he could, Wicksy was prepared to suffer a little. He got off the stool, turned, and froze.

Over by the arcade machine, a few feet to the right of the pool table, two middle-aged men were talking. They weren't anything like the other crowd though, the ones huddled at the end of the bar. These two were hawk-eyed and fit looking. And Wicksy recognized one of them. He was one of Benson's collectors, a Scotsman called Bryce. He usually drove the green Toyota Wicksy made a point of avoiding.

'What's up, Simon?'

Wicksy swallowed, turned his face away from the two men.

'You've gone all white,' Beckie said. There was no concern in her voice, though it had a trace of curiosity. 'What is it?'

'I think I need a change of atmosphere. This place always makes me feel funny after a bit. Too stuffy.'

'You mean you want to leave?'

'Yeah.'

'But we've only just got here.' There was a petulant note in Beckie's voice now. 'Why don't you just stand outside for a minute? Get some fresh air into you. Then you can come back in.'

'No, it's the place,' Wicksy said. 'It goes for me.'

Were they watching him, those two? Had they been

43

tailing him? Benson had said there was no way to stay out of his reach. Was this an act of proof, or was it going to be something else, a showdown maybe? A hard warning, at best. They sure as hell weren't here by coincidence.

'If the place makes you feel so bad why did you come?'

'To please you. You wanted to come here. But I can't stick it any longer.'

'Oh, is that right?' Beckie was glaring. 'You just happen to get an attack of claustrophobia the minute I mention I want to say hello to Linda. Amazing. If you don't want to talk to her why don't you just say so?'

Wicksy stole one sharp, momentary glance across the room. He felt his heart clench. *Bryce was looking at him!*

'Come on, Beckie. We're gettin' out of here.'

As he caught her arm Beckie twisted it free. She looked angry. Wicksy reached for her again and she stepped back.

'Beckie, we're *goin*'!'

'You can go if you like. I'm staying.'

'But how will you get home?'

'Somebody'll give me a lift,' Beckie snapped. 'I've never had any trouble getting transport.'

Wicksy stood for a second, looking helplessly at her, feeling his wretchedness seep through him like sickly sweat.

'I just don't understand you, Simon.'

That sounded final. Beckie turned and walked towards her friend. Even the way she walked made it final. Wicksy turned, saw Bryce one more time, caught the chilling look, the reminder that to this man violence was a way of life, a profession. He couldn't be warned off like one of the silly old farts at the end of the bar. Feeling himself begin to shake and lose his co-ordination, Wicksy strode to the door and shouldered it open. He stepped into the night air, feeling it close around him like sanctuary. He headed for the car, fumbled the key in the lock and on the third try got it open. As he bent to get in he heard the pub door creak open behind him. He tried, but he couldn't make himself climb into the car.

Slowly he turned, ready to see the shape coming at him, ready to be even more frightened and perhaps hurt. But it was a girl who had come out of the pub. She was walking towards a car parked on the other side of the doorway.

Wicksy slid into the driving seat and drew the door shut. He sat with his head back for a second, hearing his shaky breathing in the padded space. Five days to the 7th, and already he was beginning to crack up. He was losing every grip and foothold on the real world. He'd even lost his girlfriend. Was this what happened? Did every poor sod in this kind of trap find himself being stripped of comforts, even the tiniest, before he stepped into the jaws of whatever hell the Bensons of the world held in store?

In the darkness Wicksy put the key in the ignition, wishing, as he had before but more fiercely now, that he had a father, or a mother, or *somebody* to turn to and confess his terror.

Thursday

'This stuff,' Percy Salter said, waving his hands over the instruments set out on the floor of his shop, 'has a problem attached to it. To all of it.' He shook his bald little head, as if he were reluctant to say what the problem was. 'Two problems, come to think of it.' His mouth clamped shut suddenly and he shook his head several times, making his wattles flap. 'Let's not beat about the bush. Three problems, and they're serious.'

'But it's good stuff,' Wicksy said. 'It's all in good working order. You can check it out.'

'I would anyway. If it wasn't working there'd be four problems.'

'So tell me,' Wicksy sighed.

'The name, for a start. Every piece is the same make, and that make just isn't in. It's dated. Kids don't want the logo seen on their instruments.'

'But the stuff's hardly any age . . .'

'Makes no difference,' Percy said. 'Shiftin' that label is like floggin' bacon sandwiches in Golders Green. Nobody wants to know. So all this gear would hang about the shelves, takin' up valuable space. God knows how long it would be before I could move it. So that's one serious problem, right? Another one is, it's not compatible.'

'Compatible?'

'With all the new add-ons that are comin' along. Standardization's the thing now. In a space of three months I've seen it take shape right before my eyes. Everythin' has to be compatible with everythin' else. If you've a system that's outside the standard you're stuck. Snookered. Look what happened with videos. Nothin' wrong with Betamax, was there? But it wasn't flavour of the month and suddenly VHS was the standard.' Percy waved a despairing hand at the instruments. 'Musical Betamax, this lot. Good stuff, sound as a pound, but nobody touches that system any more.'

Wicksy wished he had never brought the stuff along. He hadn't wanted to part with it anyway. He still didn't, because he had seen it as a lifeline, the basis of an emergency career to whip up a few pounds doing gigs with whoever he could gather round him in a band. Except forming a band wasn't easy. Not when you had the name of being a bloke who screwed things up, who hadn't the necessary charisma to make a band work. That morning, on an impulse powered by a need to do *something* to help himself, he had loaded the gear into the car and brought it along to Percy, who had sold it to him in the first place.

'Problem number three is the condition it's in. I know second-hand stuff can't be expected to have the sheen of brand-new tackle. But I mean – look at it. It's taken a lot of knocks, son. Be fair, it looks like it's been through a hell of a lot since the day it was made.'

Wicksy had warned the lads about that. But they hadn't listened. Onstage any old finish looked good, thanks to the coloured lights. In daylight it was a different story. The lads had treated the equipment roughly. When they dismantled the synthesiser and amps after a gig they always did it as if they were pulling scaffolding apart, ripping out plugs and heaving the components into the back of whatever dirty hired van they happened to be using. Lying there on Percy's carpeted floor, the instruments looked scuffed and drab.

'So what kind of figure would you put on it?' Wicksy said. 'I know I can't expect anythin' like I paid for it, of course . . .'

'How much were you hopin' for?' Percy asked evasively.

Wicksy hadn't thought of a figure. If Harry hadn't overloaded one of the amps, and consequently ruined not only the amp itself but a keyboard and tape unit as well, there might have been a tidy few quid in the deal. As it was, the few pieces here didn't look as if they were worth much. Maybe three hundred pounds, Wicksy thought tentatively.

'Four hundred quid,' he told Percy.

'What?' The little man looked startled, as if someone had given him terrible news. 'Four hundred? Did I hear you right? Christ, I'm in business. I'm not a charity.'

'Well . . .'

'Look, I've told you what's wrong with the stuff.'

'What sort of price would you say, then?'

'I'll be straight with you.' Percy put the fingertips of both hands to his temples as he surveyed the instruments again. 'Bearin' in mind the label's a drug on the market, an' that the stuff isn't compatible with any of the new add-ons an' accessories, an' also bearin' in mind it looks like it's been left out in the open for a month, I'd say it's worth . . . oh, say sixty quid.'

For a second Wicksy thought he had picked it up wrong. But when he re-ran it he heard the same figure.

'That's a lot less than I – '

'It's a lot more than I should offer you,' Percy cut in. 'I shouldn't make you any offer at all. But we've done business in the past an' I've a certain loyalty to my clients – which doesn't do my business any good, I can tell you. Take it or leave it, son. I can't do any better than sixty. I wouldn't give my own mother more for this lot.'

Five minutes later Wicksy climbed back into the car with six tenners in his pocket and a bleak, cold sensation somewhere between his stomach and his head. Everything, he believed, had finally fallen through.

Driving back to Ilford he gazed at people on the streets, other traffic, children playing in a park, all the time feeling he was cut off from them. He had gone over to the limbo reserved for those about to meet disaster head on. The instruments, he realized now, had been held in reserve as an answer, one to be turned to when other options had been exhausted. The idea of getting up another band had been fanciful; what he had really been doing was holding on to a final card. And now it had turned out to be a joker. Wicksy needed no further proof that he was on the worst losing streak he'd ever known. He was no coward, but he felt like crying.

Sid Benson spent half an hour every Thursday morning behind the locked doors of a pub near the centre of Ilford where it was rumoured, by people who never dared use the place, that every well-heeled villain in London turned up at one time or another. The rumours, like most of the long-standing variety, had become fictionalized to a wild extent, but it was certainly true that the proportion of God-fearing law-abiders to rogues using the pub had been similar, over the years, to the ratio of foreigners to native British to be found most days in the Tower of London.

Sid was half-owner of the pub. His partner was a seasoned publican, Big Jack Tracey, a man who got on with his job and left Sid to pursue his own various callings. The partnership of a straight, rather gentle big victualler and Sid Benson seemed odd to most people except the partners themselves. They had been boyhood pals and

49

had even done their National Service together. Ties stronger than actual brotherhood had brought them together in this business, financed in the beginning by Sid, who found it a useful place to conduct business meetings.

Today, while Big Jack was downstairs in the cellar cleaning his pipes, Sid and his principal lieutenant, Ian Bryce, sat at a table near the bar. Thursday was the day to talk about the state of the money-lending business. The agenda, on this occasion, was brief. On the table by Ian Bryce's right hand was a notebook full of terse notations about the progress of eighteen current, so-far trouble-free transactions. By his left hand was a piece of paper with nothing on it but initials. Ian's shorthand method was primitive, but it did keep the business paperwork to a manageable size – and it was highly secure, since only he knew what most of it meant.

'One thing,' Sid said, 'before we get to anything else. A man who tapped the mechanic at Gibson's Garage for a ton three weeks ago has decided he doesn't want to give it back. He's denying he ever borrowed the money.'

'So?' Bryce's face was flat and expressionless, like his voice, which betrayed nothing except that he came from Glasgow. 'It's no' a problem of yours, is it?'

'Not at all,' Sid agreed. 'But I like that mechanic. He's a good man, does a fine job on my car, never gets above himself. He's not the type who can call in a debt except by pleading. That's not going to work for him in this case. His boss had a word with me and I said I'd do what I could.'

Bryce nodded. 'I see. Whit's the target's details?'

Sid pushed forward a piece of paper with a name and a Fulham address written on it. Bryce transferred the details, in bafflingly truncated form, to the paper by his left hand.

'Send somebody,' Sid grunted. 'Don't take up your own time on it.' He yawned and stretched, then put his palms flat on the table. 'Right. Business.'

'Good news first.' Bryce touched the open notebook, his head hovering over it for a moment as he checked his facts. 'Eighteen transactions runnin' smooth. Two of them looked shaky last week but they've come into line. All it took was a couple of words. Three should complete on the next payment, another five on the one after that. The two long-term jobs are bein' monitored. They look sound enough, for now.'

'Uhuh.' Sid put his hands behind his head. 'How about the naughty boys?'

'Eight.' Bryce tapped the sheet of paper on his left. 'Two of them went critical, if you get my drift.'

'Action?'

Bryce cleared his throat. 'On Monday the butcher had an accident an' cut his arm open. Real bad, it was. We took him chocolates to the hospital an' promised him his knife might slip again, in the region of his weddin' tackle. The carpet-layer was stupid enough to nail his hand to a floor . . .'

'I've an awful feeling we'll lose on that one,' Sid said. 'Well, not lose, exactly . . .'

'He paid back the original eight hundred plus two hundred an' fifty of the interest,' Bryce murmured, consulting the notebook by way of cross-reference. 'But I think he's strapped as bad as anybody can get. His partner runnin' off like he did, just after we made the loan, an' emptyin' the bank account before he went . . .' Bryce shrugged. 'Ah fancy all the carpet-layer's good for is a warnin' to the wayward.'

'Fair enough. But make sure he doesn't think he's

51

getting off light. I don't want anybody saying we're going soft.'

Bryce ran a finger down the other initials. 'The supermarket manager's on his second warnin'. So are the greengrocer an' the security man at Fletcher's. Our pal the ticket tout had to be nudged firmly on Tuesday night – we had a job findin' him, I think he's bein' chased by other people. I'll keep a close watch on him from now on. The bloke from the DHSS is due to fall off his bus on the way home tomorrow night – he's been slidin' back very badly on the payments.' Bryce looked up. 'That leaves the fadin' rock star.'

Sid nodded. 'Simon Wicks. It's a pity about him. He seemed like a good bet.'

'I think he was. But the arse fell out of his plans.'

'What's the status?'

'He missed three payments at odd times,' Bryce said. 'His argument was good an' the prospects of him comin' into line again each time were good, too. He lived up to expectation, but of course the extra interest put a strain on him. Then he spoke to Willie, who's been takin' his payments, an' asked for a time extension on the payment that was due last Monday. Willie gave him till next Monday and came straight to me – to alert me, like. So we've done a bit of nosin'. It doesn't look good. I'd say he's startin' to panic.'

'Which would be fine, if the panic juiced up his ingenuity a bit.'

'Exactly,' Bryce said. 'But I don't reckon he's got anywhere to turn.'

'We'll see what happens on Monday, then. If he pays up he can have a stern warning that there'll be no more extensions. If he doesn't have the readies . . .' Sid stared at the table. 'What do you reckon?'

'He's a good-lookin' boy,' Bryce said thoughtfully. 'I think what we should do is lay on a warnin' before the due date. Just to keep the pressure on, an' remind him we're close at hand. If he still turns up with nothin' on Monday, I fancy it would be in order to do a wee modifyin' job on the good looks.'

'Sounds reasonable to me.'

Sid watched Bryce put a mark on his sheet of paper, then fold it into a notebook and pocket the lot, signalling the end of the proceedings for this week. Sid looked at his watch.

'If that's it, Ian, I think I'll get Big Jack to brew me one of his fancy Italian coffees.'

'I think I'll join ye,' Bryce said. 'It's a bit early for a pint, isn't it?'

Late that afternoon, as he was brewing a cup of tea at Pat's place, Wicksy remembered a story he'd once heard about a musical instrument dealer in the West End. It was a story that made him glumly certain he'd been heftily ripped off over the sale of the band's gear.

It had been an acquaintance, Gary, who had found himself tight for cash and decided to sell his beloved Spanish guitar. He took it to the West End dealer and asked what it was worth. The dealer looked at the guitar with the face of a man contemplating something terrible. It was an unheard-of make, he said, which would create sales-resistance right from the start. On top of that the instrument was warped, there were scratches on the front board and he didn't like the look of the fret. The most he could offer for such a guitar, he regretted to say, was ten pounds. Shocked, Gary nevertheless took the money, for he was very hard up indeed.

Some days later he was approached by a friend who

actually wanted to buy his guitar from him. Gary explained that he had already sold it, but added that his friend should go to the musical instrument dealer who had bought the guitar, because he was likely to get a bargain there, considering how little the dealer had paid. So the friend went to the shop and asked the man, as casually as he could, if he happened to have a second-hand Spanish guitar for sale. 'You're in luck,' the dealer said, pointing proudly to Gary's guitar hanging prominently on the wall behind the counter. 'It's yours for sixty pounds, and I'm robbing myself.' Gary's friend was appalled. He told the man he thought the price was way too high, to which the dealer retorted, 'Have you any idea how scarce those models are?'

Pat came through from her bedroom while Wicksy was still stinging over the way he had been treated.

'Nice to see your smilin' fizzog brightenin' up my kitchen.'

Wicksy shot her a baleful look. 'Give me one reason to smile an' I'll do it.'

'How about if I tell you a joke?' Pat made a one-sided grin as she swayed by the drainer, already half-drunk in preparation for a night out with a couple of friends.

'I'd rather you didn't. Your jokes depress me.'

'This one won't. I promise. A punter's girlfriend told him it.' Pat frowned, trying to remember how the joke began. 'Yeah, got it. Can you tell me where the British Standard kite mark is on a condom?'

Wicksy stared at her.

'Well?' Pat prompted. 'Can you tell me where it is?'

Wicksy shook his head.

'You can't? Well, you don't roll one up very far, do you?'

Her laugh was sandpaper on Wicksy's discomfort. What

other mother, he wondered, would regularly tell her son dirty jokes?'

The old bag isn't my mother.

'Oh, you're turnin' into a right dry stick,' Pat wheezed, her laugh tailing off. 'You've got to shake yourself out of all this broodiness, Simon. You know what'll happen if you don't? You'll get over your problems, but by the time you do you'll have turned into one of them twenty-year-old middle-aged men. There's a lot of them about.' She belched softly and slapped her fingers to her lips. 'I see them all the time. Lost their capacity for fun, only want to find somethin' to moan over or go silent about. It's no way to – '

'Listen. With half the worry I've got you'd be on your knees howlin' up the chimney. You keep makin' out it's somethin' trivial an' I should just let it pass over my head. But it won't do that, can't you understand? It's more likely to pass *through* my head an' do a lot of damage on the way.'

'All right, all right . . .' Pat made a placating gesture. 'I'll say no more about it.'

'Ta.'

'There was somethin' else I wanted to talk to you about, anyway.' Pat took a cigarette from a packet on the drainer and lit it with a bright orange plastic lighter. 'This do I'm goin' to tonight, it's for Steph's birthday. Gonna be a surprise for her.'

'That should be fun,' Wicksy said flatly. 'You should have given her some warnin', though, so she could get herself up in her finery.'

He recalled a couple of lines from a lyric he had written once, for a sloppy ballad aimed at a girl he fancied at the time: *Dazzling girl in your party dress, Loveliest here I must confess* . . . He tried to imagine Steph decked out to match the lines and he nearly laughed.

'You shouldn't be hard on Steph,' Pat chided. 'It's not her fault she's got no sense of fashion. That girl has a heart of gold.'

'Yeah. Cold an' yellow.'

'Oh come on, Simon. She thinks the world of you.'

'That's another thing that gets me down.'

'What?'

'The strange power I have over scraggy old birds.'

Oddly, Pat didn't seem needled. Drunk or sober, she usually flew to the defence of her friends.

'Well, whatever you think of her, she's got a birthday today an' we're goin' to celebrate it. I saved up a few quid an' got her ever such a nice locket. Silver, it is. Well, plated.'

Wicksy looked at the dregs in his cup. 'Is this what you wanted to talk to me about?'

'Yeah.'

A quick glance at her face told him plenty. The small forward jerk of the chin, the fleeting, unavoidable deflection of the eyes. She was up to something.

'What I didn't budget for, you see, was that the rest of the crowd decided we'd go up West. Majority decision, I'd no choice.'

'You could've chosen not to go,' Wicksy said.

'What? Not go to my mate's birthday do? What kind of friend would that make me?'

Wicksy didn't know if he felt surprised by what was about to come, or if he simply knew that he should never expect more than censure or scrounging from this woman.

'If you can't afford a thing, Mum, you can't afford it. It's somethin' you've told me more than once, isn't it?'

'This is different,' Pat said, with the hint of a whine.

56

'You have to make sacrifices for your friends.'

'Who has to? You or me?'

'Me.'

Wicksy narrowed an eye at her.

'What I mean is, if you lend me a few bob, I'll give it back. So the sacrifice, in the end, is mine, right?'

'What makes you think I've any money? You know how I'm fixed. I've got my sosh an' the pittance Jacko pays me. That's my whole income.'

Pat now adopted the Wounded Madonna look, as Wicksy called it. Her eyes puckered with simulated pain and her shoulders sagged. She let out a tiny sigh.

'It's not as if I was goin' to ask you to lend me a fortune,' she murmured. 'Just enough to let me stand my corner, that's all.'

'It'll be some corner if you're goin' up West. An' it won't stop at rounds of drinks, will it? What's the bettin' you'll all wind up in an Indian or a Chinky?'

It was time for a stiff silence. Pat walked to the window and stood there with her arms folded, staring out at the side of the house next door. Wicksy knew he could simply walk out and leave her in a fix. He also knew that Pat had a talent for knowing when she could pull this act and get away with it. He waited, feeling nothing for the moment, waiting for the pained accusations. Pat's preliminary intake of breath came after about a minute.

'You can be very hard, Simon. Unfeeling.' She continued to look out of the window as she spoke. 'I brought you up, remember. I shielded you all through your childhood.'

Wicksy wondered how she could have the gall to talk that way. His childhood, his and his brother's, had been a succession of upheavals and ghastly revelations about adult behaviour that no child could ever have deserved.

But this was old Pat talking, he reminded himself. She was capable of saying anything. Her life was governed by calculations, not principles.

'When you couldn't find anywhere to live, I didn't hesitate to let you come here. An' you're still here.'

Allowed to stay so long as I pay an extortionate rent, Wicksy thought. *And I stay because I've nowhere else to go – otherwise I wouldn't come near the place.*

'I've put myself out for you, not just now but for years an' years. Yet when I ask you for a loan, a tiny loan that I've every intention of payin' back, you turn me down flat. That's hurtful, Simon, very hurtful.'

And of course he would give her the money, because he happened to have some on him. It was too little to help with his debt, anyway, and although he saw through Pat clearer than he could see through glass, he bore a thread of compassion for her that dictated he should help her whenever it didn't hurt him to do so.

'Finished?' he said.

'Yes,' Pat sighed. 'I've finished.'

'How much do you want?'

Still facing the window Pat said, 'I don't want anythin' off you if it's not freely given.'

'Could you spare me any more bullshit an' just tell me what you want?'

Pat turned, her face struggling for huffy rectitude.

'I'll want it back, mind,' Wicksy said, not to make himself seem too much of a soft touch.

'Twenty should cover it,' Pat murmured. 'Or maybe make it twenty-five, to be safe.'

'Here.' Wicksy finger-counted three ten-pound notes in his hip pocket and drew them out. 'Take thirty. I've no fives.'

'Cheers.' Pat took the money with a shy little smile. 'Sorry if I went on a bit . . .'

'Forget it.'

The front door knocker rattled as Pat was tucking the money into her handbag. She and Wicksy looked at each other.

'You expectin' anybody?' Pat said.

Wicksy shook his head.

'Neither am I.'

'So somebody's called unexpected. It happens.'

Pat scowled and went out into the hall. Wicksy heard the door open. There was a moment's silence, then a man's voice rumbled. The door closed again and Pat came back, followed by Wicksy's stepfather, Brian.

'Nice little family scene,' he said, nodding to Wicksy. He crossed the kitchen and stood by the cooker, one hand resting on the top, the other in his pocket. It was a stance Wicksy remembered from childhood, the pose of a seedy monarch about to address his worn-down subjects. 'No sign of the third member, though. Isn't he about?'

'We haven't heard from David in a while,' Pat said. 'Keeps himself to himself these days. Some people should follow his example.'

'Oh . . .' Brian raised his eyebrows. 'Tongue as sharp as ever, eh, Pat?' He was drunk but trying to conceal it. 'You'll slice your face off with it one of these days.'

'You said you wanted a quick word.' Pat folded her arms. 'Have it, will you? I'm gettin' ready to go out.'

'Out on the town, eh?' Brian's eyes darted round the room. 'I get the feelin' of, wossname, *affluence* comin' off you these days, Pat. I saw you on the street a while back an' you looked smart, well-fed, well-dressed. I look at the house, spick an' span with a lot of new bits an' bobs here

59

an' there, an' I say to myself, this girl's doin' all right for herself.'

'Are you here to scrounge money?' Pat demanded.

'I'm here about my bloody rights, Pat.'

Wicksy grunted softly. Brian stared at him. The thin pretence of friendliness had evaporated. Brian went on staring as Wicksy moved to the table and rested his buttock on the edge. It was a deliberate move of confrontation, scaled to remind Brian that he was a guest here, and should mind his mouth.

'Rights?' Pat squeaked. 'What rights have you got where I'm concerned? What're you on about?'

'Insurance,' Brian said. 'That's what I'm on about.'

Wicksy saw the momentary evasion on Pat's face – the averted eyes, the jerking chin. It passed swiftly and she was glaring at Brian again.

'I've no idea what you mean.'

'Well listen an' I'll explain. One night not long ago, when I was just sittin' with a pint an' lettin' old times run through my head, suddenly somethin' went ping! an' I thought harder, really concentrated, an' after a minute I remembered it clear as day.' He pointed at Wicksy. 'Remember when he was just a nipper, a bloke at the door talked you into takin' out an insurance policy on him an' his brother? Two policies, Pat. Both to mature when the lads turned twenty.'

'I remember about them, yeah,' Pat said. 'So what?'

'Well Simon here's twenty now, an' David's about a year older.'

'And?'

'So I reckon you've collected on both policies. That'd explain the flash, the affluent touches. An' since it was my wages that paid a fair bit of the premiums on them policies, I fancy I'm due a cut.'

'You're a right heap of tat, aren't you?' Wicksy said.

'Shut it,' Brian warned, keeping his eyes on Pat.

'Like hell I'll shut it.' Wicksy stood away from the table. 'Is there nothin' you wouldn't do to grab some cash you've never earned? You're a scum bag, know that?'

When Brian was drunk, one level of emotion tended to shortcut to another, usually missing some stages on the way. There was no process of change, no pause as one gear slid through the ratios to change his impetus. In a flash he was in front of Wicksy, staring into his eyes, breathing onions on him.

'Watch your gob, smart-arse!'

'An' you watch yours!' Wicksy shouted, making Brian wince at the noise. 'Why don't you just piss off an' get on with your million-quid statuette scheme? A soddin' tycoon like you shouldn't be wastin' his time tryin' to blackmail pin money out of the ex-wife he wasn't halfways fit to support in the first place!'

Brian grabbed the neck of Wicksy's sweater. Wicksy's left hand came up and the fingers closed round Brian's knuckles. Having located, they tightened. Caution took the irate sparkle from Brian's eyes.

'Just let go,' Wicksy said, softly now, making the tendons of Brian's hand grind against each other. 'If you don't, neither will I.'

Brian's response was to try kneeing Wicksy in the crotch. Which Wicksy had expected. He jack-knifed back, still clutching Brian's hand. The attacking knee thrust upwards, met nothing but air and was held from beneath by Wicksy's free hand. He tightened the fingers of both hands, simultaneously sending intense pain down Brian's calf and making his knuckles crunch.

'Bastard!' Brian tried to wrench himself free.

'Leave him Simon!' Pat yelped.

Wicksy was in a position that wouldn't allow him to do anything but go forward. He had Brian in a dual grip, which promised spectacular results. Before delivering the *coup de grâce* he put his face very close to the victim's.

'When you leave here,' he said, 'go an' adopt a pimp as a brother. Then you'll have somebody to look up to.'

Brian drew his head back sharply, sending a clear warning of what he intended to do. He had never done it before and that showed, too.

'Try it, ferret-face!'

Wicksy grabbed a tendon and a nerve in a pinch-grip at the side of Brian's knee. He squeezed and twisted, and as Brian roared Wicksy jerked the captive hand sideways at the wrist. At precisely the right moment he released Brian, letting him fall back against the cooker with a crash. He tried to take a lunging step at his attacker and found his outraged leg wouldn't hold him. He landed on the floor, still yelling.

Pat had flattened herself against the 'fridge. Pub violence was something she took in her stride, but the domestic variety held too many daunting echoes.

'Time to go,' Wicksy said. He bent and took Brian's jacket by the collar and one sleeve. With a jerk he got him to his feet and shoved him out into the hallway.

'You'll bloody pay for this!'

'Yeah, yeah.'

At the door Wicksy let go of Brian and turned the lock. In a sudden flurry of arms and clockworking legs Brian shot back along the hall to the kitchen. Wicksy, thrown for a second, heard Pat scream. There was a loud slap of flesh on flesh, then another. Wicksy ran to the kitchen and got there as the back door slammed.

'God almighty . . .'

Pat was sitting on the floor, her legs sticking out in

front of her. She was staring straight ahead, stunned. There was a purpling weal on her left cheek.

Wicksy helped her up into a chair by the table.

'He's an animal, Mum. You should never have let him in. Sit tight an' I'll make you a cup of tea.'

'You shouldn't have provoked him like that,' Pat moaned, wincing as she fingered her throbbing cheek.

'I put him in his place,' Wicksy pointed out. 'You have to with characters like him. If you don't, they just walk all over you.'

'That's the trouble. He'll come back here an' have another go at me when I'm on my own. He's that kind of man, Simon. He's vindictive. You made him look a wally so now he'll seethe about it until he gets even.'

'But it's me he wants to get even with,' Wicksy said, filling the kettle. 'If he thinks he's got a beef, I'm the one to bring it to.'

'He knows he can't do that.' Pat groaned. 'I'll be the one he goes for. He always has done.' She stood and went to the mirror by the side of the sink. 'Oh my God! How can I go out lookin' like this?'

Wicksy lit the gas and put the kettle down over the flames. He turned to Pat, frowning.

'All that about the insurance policies – was he right about it?'

'The policies were my business,' Pat snapped, going back to the table and sitting down. 'I kept them goin' over the years. I was entitled to benefit.'

'But what about David an' me? Shouldn't we have had some of it? I'd have thought that's why you took the insurance out – to help us along at a time when we might need a few bob.'

It was dawning on Wicksy that the money might have been available at the *precise* time he'd needed it to update the band's equipment. The whole set-up would have fallen through just the same, but at least he wouldn't have been lumbered with the trouble he was in now.

'The way I see it,' Pat said, 'I scrimped an' saved all my married life. I sacrificed myself for you an' your brother. I got damned little in return. So when the time came for the policies to cough up the jackpot, I felt I was entitled to every penny.'

'I never even guessed you'd come into money. You kept it quiet enough.'

'Listen Simon, I've learned my lesson over the years. You don't let anybody know when you're flush. People are like vultures. Even your nearest an' dearest will be at you, tryin' to tap you if they think there's half a chance.'

Like today, Wicksy thought, when she'd been quite prepared to blackmail him for a loan. A loan that would be written off if he didn't badger her for it back.

'There wasn't so much cash, anyway,' Pat went on.

'How much, exactly?' Wicksy said, spooning tea into the pot.

'Not a lot at all.'

Wicksy stared, making it clear he wanted a precise answer.

'Your policy paid six hundred an' odd.'

'How long did it take you to blow that lot?'

'It's 1985, Simon,' Pat said sharply. 'Six hundred's practically nothin'. It ain't no fortune, that's for sure. There was things I needed. Things for the house mostly. This place don't run itself, you know.'

'Yeah,' Wicksy sighed. 'I know.'

Allowing for Pat's usual revisions of uncomfortable truths, he decided there still hadn't been enough cash to make any real difference to his circumstances. Even if she had given him half, he would still have had to borrow. It was a bleak consolation.

'What with that, an' the money you got from David's policy, you must've been pretty well set up for a while there.'

'For once in me life,' Pat said, touching her cheek again.

Wicksy looked at her, seeing how pathetic she looked, her hair dishevelled, make-up smudged and a big bruise spreading along her cheek. His compassion for the poor, hurting woman inside her was keen at that moment. If only he could touch that person and offer some comfort. And perhaps draw some, he thought wistfully.

Friday

Visitors to the Ginger Giant were confronted by three doors, all of them leading into the public bar. This was often perplexing, especially if a newcomer had accepted an invitation to meet a friend in the lounge. There were no signs in the bar to indicate where the lounge was, and more than one bewildered soul had left the place believing he had gone to the wrong pub. In fact the lounge door was located behind a jutting, square-edged pillar at the end of the public bar. The lounge was a small room, nylon-carpeted in orange and brown, with six tables, eighteen chairs, a crescent bar and dim yellow lights suspended in three clusters of four from the dusty, sculpted-plaster ceiling. The walls were covered with green flock curlicues on a cream background.

Nobody liked to work in the lounge. Its elements added up to something depressing, an atmosphere of hopelessness that managed, sooner or later, to permeate the jolliest company. The room, Wicksy had told Jacko, was a bit like the waiting room at a chapel of rest. Jacko replied that he thought it was a nice little lounge, even though he couldn't have failed to notice that people usually avoided it, unless privacy was crucially important.

'It's got class, that room,' Jacko asserted. 'As good as anythin' you'll find this side of Watford.'

That Friday lunchtime Wicksy had drawn the short straw. The lounge was open because office girls in the district who liked to have an end-of-week drink also liked to enjoy the event unembarrassed by the remarks of the local gentry who used the public bar. In the lounge the most uncomfortable thing likely to happen would be that Jacko would come in to clear the glasses and, simultaneously, hand out his leaden flattery to the young women at the tables.

'He's creepy,' one girl had warned her friends. 'Listenin' to his patter's like bein' touched up with wet rubber gloves.'

In daylight the lounge was less dispiriting than it was during the evening, but Wicksy still hated going in there. The room accommodated his gloom too neatly, creating the feeling that things weren't only pretty bad, but would get worse.

There was a good-sized crowd in, which helped. Wicksy was too busy to let the room get to him. He had even begun to enjoy himself, exchanging wisecracks and good-humoured ribbing with the customers, until a Beer Hero turned up at the bar, ready to put a weekend shine on his opinion of himself.

'Two halves of Oscar,' he called to Wicksy, 'a pint of Gary an' a half of Mick with a touch of lemonade in it.'

Wicksy looked at him. He was maybe twenty-eight, fashionably short-haired though it didn't suit him, grinning across at the girls on his table as he spoke. He wore a blazer and his tie was loosened, declaring his present disdain for the rules of office propriety.

'I didn't catch that,' Wicksy said.

Beer Heroes were a pain, especially when they'd hit saturation, as this man had. Wicksy had seen him come in, three pints ago, and he had looked positively shy. But the beer changed everything. Now he was Clarke Kent out of the phone booth, ready to dazzle and astonish with his hitherto concealed talent.

'I thought I said it plain enough,' the Hero drawled,

grinning again at his companions. 'It's two halves of Oscar, right? Then a pint of Gary – '

'Hold it right there.' Wicksy came close, resting his forearms on the bar. 'Why don't you stop prattin' about an' let me have your order, eh?'

The Hero blinked, still unaware that he was causing irritation.

'I *was* giving you my order.'

'I didn't understand it.'

The Hero turned to his friends and spread his hands in amazement. Wicksy turned, too, and walked to the opposite end of the bar where he served another customer. When he came back the Hero was looking annoyed.

'Right then, we'll start again,' Wicksy said. 'What can I get you?'

'I thought you were a Londoner,' the Hero said.

'I am. What's that got to do with anythin'?'

'Rhyming slang, that's what. I thought you'd have known. A Gary's a Gary Glitter – bitter. Oscar's an Oscar Wilde – mild. When I asked for a half of Mick – '

'You meant a Mick Jagger, which is a lager, yeah?' Again Wicksy leaned close. He spoke very softly, so only the Hero would hear. 'Look, I choose not to recognize all that jabber, OK? It's a hard enough job workin' back here without havin' to put up with show-offs paradin' their knowledge of quaint Cockney lingo. Plain English is just fine in this place. Now.' He stood back, picking up a glass. 'Your order was?'

Discomfited, the Hero stated his requirements and broodily dug out his loose change.

'Nice to meet a friendly barman,' he grunted as he paid up.

'An' it's a novelty to come across a tit with a blazer on,' Wicksy said brightly as he took the money.

If nothing else, the small exchange had taken his mind off himself. Now, as he mopped the bartop with a cloth, he realized that to a man whose time was running out, the little blips in a daily routine could offer something like relief, no matter how unpleasant they were. Perhaps, he thought, they were the equivalent of banging the knee on something sharp, momentarily shifting your attention from a toothache.

He looked up from mopping, saw a man come into the lounge, and wondered about something else: could words like 'toothache', when they were run through the mind in a certain way, actually conjure their equivalent right before a bloke's eyes? A toothache had certainly put in an appearance, right on cue, in the form of Brian Wicks. He sauntered heavily towards the bar, moving his shoulders like somebody dangerous.

'Yes?' Wicksy said without moving his lips.

'I want a word with you.'

'I'm here to sell drinks.'

'Give me a half of bitter then.'

Wicksy pulled the drink and put it on the bar. He took Brian's money, all shrapnel, twos and fives, and dropped it in the till.

'Right,' Brian said when he had taken a sip. 'A warnin', now I've had time to think things out.'

'Don't threaten me,' Wicksy murmured. 'I'm tellin' you this straight. No matter what you've sat in a corner an' convinced yourself you can do, if you put even the hint of a threat on me I'll come over that bar an' lay you out. Just drink your beer an' depart as if you were civilized.'

'It's no threat I'm makin',' Brian said.

'Don't tell me – it's a promise, yeah?'

'If you'll shut up an' listen . . .'

Brian did a sideways slide of his upper and lower teeth

69

across each other, making a sound like a fingernail on the teeth of a comb. Wicksy put his hands on the bar and leaned on his extended arms, waiting.

'Right,' Brian said, 'this is a fair warnin'. I'm takin' the business of the insurance policies further. I know my rights. I contributed to the payments over the years. Now if your mother did herself a bit of good out of the proceeds – an' I'll lay even money she did – I'm goin' to do the same. I'm warnin' you to warn her.'

'You seriously want a cut?'

'Too bloody right I do. It's only fair.'

'An' of course you've always believed in doin' things the fair way.' Wicksy shook his head. 'You're talking through a hole in the top of your head, do you know that? You've got no rights there. It wasn't no legal financial agreement you got involved in. Mum did the signin', remember. You never wanted to sign anythin'. So it was a couple of policies that matured an' the company paid out – to Mum. You weren't there with your hands cupped ready for some of the bunce, so you didn't get any an' nobody can prove you were entitled. I was supposed to be entitled but I got nothin' either. I'm not bitchin' about it. There's no point.'

'But there *is* a point, I've thought it out, like I said – '

'Why don't you save your mental powers for workin' on a decent, down-to-earth scheme for earnin' some cash, instead of clutchin' at straws?'

'Why don't you take a warnin', like I told you?'

Wicksy smiled at the bar. 'Tell you what – go an' see a lawyer or somebody like that. Ask him how you stand.'

'I'm talkin' about a *moral* right here,' Brian said. 'Nothin' to do with the law. I'm entitled, I know I'm entitled, an' I'm goin' to get what I'm due – if I've to take it out of your old lady's hide.'

'Oh, yeah, of course. Takin' your moral rights out of a woman.' Wicksy clucked his tongue softly, giving Brian time to read his face and see how much he despised him. 'She reckoned you'd be capable of doin' somethin' along them lines.'

'Believe it.'

'But what happens when I catch up with you? Thought that one out, have you?'

'I've got mates,' Brian said, trying to make it sound like the darkest of warnings.

'You'll never have a mate as long as you've a bleached raisin for a brain – an' that really means never.'

Now Brian tried another stance that didn't sit well on him. He beckoned Wicksy close with a curling finger, at the same time baring his teeth at him. Wicksy responded by smiling patiently, the way he would at a tiny puppy snarling round his ankles. He leaned forward, inclining an ear.

'I can get you done over any time I want.'

'It'd be a neat double,' Wicksy said lightly. 'Thumpin' your ex-wife an' gettin' your stepson done over. Nice, that.' He stood upright abruptly, making Brian jump. 'I warned you what I'd do if you threatened me. Now you've done it an' I'm tellin' you – if you're not out that door in ten seconds flat I'm comin' over there.'

'I'm entitled to finish my beer.' Brian snatched up the glass.

'You're dead fond of that word "entitled", aren't you?' Wicksy grabbed the sleeve of the hand holding the glass and shook it, splashing beer over Brian's knuckles. 'There. You've had half the beer. Do you want the other half you're entitled to, or will you leave it?'

'Hoi!' It was a hoarse cry, coming from behind Wicksy. 'What the hell are you playin' at?'

'Got a difficult one here, Jacko,' Wicksy said without looking round. 'Just helpin' him to make up his mind about leavin'.' Wicksy jerked Brian's arm again, spilling more beer.

'Pack that in!' Jacko hissed, coming forward.

Wicksy took the glass with his free hand, sliding it from Brian's sopping fingers before he released the jacket sleeve.

'Now push off,' he said.

Jacko stood gaping as Brian mopped his hand with a greyish handkerchief. He raised a warning finger at Wicksy then turned and strode out. Wicksy turned to Jacko.

'Sorry about that,' he said. 'Like I said, he was bein' difficult.'

'What you were doin' constitutes an assault,' Jacko said. He was red-faced, his eyes wide with censure. 'You can't go treatin' the public like that. That fella could have you charged.'

'Not a chance. He's got more reasons to keep clear of the law than go complainin' to them.'

Jacko's eyes narrowed suddenly. 'Listen – I recognized him, sort of. Isn't he your Mum's ex?'

Wicksy nodded.

'I thought so. Haven't seen him in years, but somethin' rang a bell. You got some squabble with him, then?'

'Nothin' I can't handle.'

'Not in here, you won't.' Jacko drew Simon aside, away from the direct staring of people at tables near the bar. 'I should sack you for what you just did. You know I don't tolerate troubles on the premises – or off the premises for that matter, if they affect my staff's work.'

It occurred to Wicksy just how the scene must have appeared to Jacko, a man of peace who saw every

72

aggressive move in this pub as a direct threat to his licence.

'I'm sorry, Jacko. It won't happen again.'

'It'd better not.'

At closing time Wicksy cleared up quickly and managed to get out of the pub before Jacko, still contending with the staff in the public bar, could enlarge on the seriousness of what had occurred. The streets outside felt more and more threatening as the days passed so Wicksy made straight for the cover of the Magic Vine, a wine bar that served soft drinks, coffee and snacks between the times it was open for the sale of alcohol. He hadn't been in there for a long time, because it held special memories for him, and because it wasn't cheap. But today he felt like indulging himself.

At a corner table, surrounded by potted plants and ornate, pseudo-antique Delft pottery, he sat with a double coffee and two jam doughnuts, taking stock of a life that showed increasing signs of decaying into a reeking puddle of nastiness.

When was the last time something pleasant had happened?

Meeting Beckie had been nice, Wicksy supposed, although he was already beginning to panic at that time, so the experience had been marred. Earlier than that, a lot earlier, he'd had a very happy moment in a wine bar like this one. He had been struggling with a lyric, something he did a lot, and sitting alone, over a glass of Chablis, in the fragile light of a candle in a bottle, the final two lines had come to him:

> While held by love my heart was torn,
> I truly wished I'd not been born.

73

It hadn't been one of his best. Far from that. But it was set to a tune he had half-dreamt one morning as he came slowly awake, and the lyric fitted the melody to perfection. Wicksy had never been able to explain to anyone how he had felt in that moment, putting the final touch to a creation that was entirely his own. There had been few times like that in his life, times when he felt his wholeness as a human being and couldn't doubt, while the feeling lasted, that he didn't have an important place in the throbbing life around him.

Wicksy didn't believe he would ever feel that spiritual integrity again. His life nowadays, inner and outer, was made up entirely of squalid fears and bruising realities. He moved from one degrading experience to another, sensing the finer elements of himself ooze away through the wounds in his pride and his near-dead talent.

I truly wished I'd not been born . . .

That had prophecy in it. The dominant faces in his life moved through his mind – the moneylenders, Jacko, his mother, nasty Brian – making a seedy rogue's gallery of every reason he had for longing to be no one. Even Jacko, the only benign figure in his present life, had come close to taking away his trivial, necessary job. Wicksy bit deep into a doughnut, trying not to wish he hadn't been brought into the world. For once, the sweetness didn't soothe him.

A movement by the bar made him look up. In the reddish light he saw a shape, puzzling in the gloom but definitely familiar. It was a young man, moving fast, and in a rush Wicksy realized why and he stood up, crabwalking round the table and hurrying to intercept the man as he reached the door.

'Eddie. I'm glad I caught you.'

74

Eddie didn't look glad about anything. He smiled uncomfortably and brushed a wisp of fair hair from his face.

'I just looked up an' saw you hurryin' out,' Wicksy said. 'Lucky I spotted you. How've you been?'

'Not bad. Yourself?'

'I've seen better times. Come an' sit down.'

'Well I'm in a bit of a hurry . . .'

Wicksy knew that, and he knew why. What had drawn his attention had been the way Eddie, just a shape on the edge of vision, had come in at a normal sauntering pace, stopped dead, then moved back to the door at speed. He had spotted Wicksy, that was why.

'I won't keep you long. You can't go rushin' off without havin' a word or two, eh?'

They went to a table. A girl in a French maid's apron came across and Eddie ordered a coffee.

'So tell me what's been happenin' since I last saw you,' Wicksy said, chewing on his doughnut again.

Eddie, never good at holding anyone's eye for long, took a swift reading of Wicksy's good-humoured expression and relaxed a shade.

'I've got a job in the new leisure centre. Been there a couple of months. I'm in charge of the men's sauna and solarium.' In spite of Eddie's discomfort he showed a glint of pride in his new position. 'It's a pretty responsible job an' they tell me I'm doin' fine. There's lots of chances of promotion. I could be on a very good thing in a year or two if I stick at it.'

'Oh, I'm sure you'll do that,' Wicksy said, wondering if he really was going to have a go at Eddie. 'You were always a trier, eh? Never one to give up at the first snag.'

'I'm goin' out with a new girl now, too.' It seemed Eddie wanted to keep talking, as if doing that would keep

75

Wicksy away from any discussion of their brief career together in the band. 'She's called Marie, Marie Jefford. Maybe you know her – small, no more than five feet, very well build, dark hair . . .'

'Sounds like a lot of chicks,' Wicksy said, wiping grains of sugar from his lips. 'Can't say I know her name.'

'No, well, she's not really from round here.' Eddie swallowed softly, his prominent Adam's apple rising and falling. He'd always had a rather slack, moist mouth, but Wicksy noticed now that it was dry-looking and tense. 'We've been talkin' about gettin' engaged. Can you imagine it?' Eddie forced a little laugh, high and edgy. 'Never thought I'd let a girl get me into a corner like that – but then I never knew a girl like Marie. Not ever.'

Wicksy was nodding, chewing, smiling faintly.

'She's a temp – good job, bags of variety an' people everywhere screamin' out for her services. I reckon we'll make a good team.' Eddie paused for breath. 'She says that if we get married, she wants to go on workin' for a few years, just so we can get some real security behind us before we start a family.'

'I'm pleased everythin's workin' out so well for you,' Wicksy said. He put down the stump of the doughnut and sipped his coffee. He waited as the girl brought Eddie's coffee and put it in front of him.

'How about the other lads? How're they doin'? For some reason I never see any of you around. Not till now, that is. How's the old gang doin'?'

'I don't see much of them,' Eddie said quickly. Too quickly. 'You know how it is. People drift apart, go their separate ways . . .'

'Separate ways is right.' Wicksy looked at the other doughnut, wishing now he hadn't wasted the money on it.

'The way you lot vanished, I thought you'd been kidnapped.'

Eddie did another swift face-read. 'It was all a bit confused,' he said vaguely. 'Seems ages ago, now.'

'Not that long. Just long enough for some disgustin' developments here an' there.' Wicksy smiled. 'Not goin' to ask me what's been goin' down?'

'Yeah, sure,' Eddie said. He took a swallow of coffee. 'How have you been gettin' along?'

'Terrible, since I saw you last.' Wicksy let his face harden all by itself. 'Once you an' the other three lads took off an' left me holdin' that debt, things started happenin' so fast I hardly noticed what day it was. I'd so much to do – like pullin' in all the loans I'd made, gettin' out my savin's, sellin' this an' that, just to make the payments.' He saw Eddie's face colour. 'Talk about time flyin',' he went on. 'I tell you, it seemed like no time at all until I was neck-deep in the shit. Behind on the payments, strugglin' just to live, worryin' my way from day to day with brick walls goin' up all round me. It's been an interestin' time, Eddie.' Wicksy paused. 'I wouldn't wish it on a dog. Not even one of you lot.'

'Come on now, Wicksy.' Eddie cleared his throat, sat forward in the chair. 'What happened wasn't our fault. It was circumstances, they just changed . . .'

'Right at the instant I needed help, for the very first time, you took off.'

'We'd have helped if we could have,' Eddie said feebly.

'But you *could* have. A bit of a group effort would have got this thing cleared off in no time. Four of us could have sacrificed ourselves for a few months an' wiped the slate. But no, you all saw it nice an' clear – I had the problem, so I could tackle it on my own. Great.'

'We were sorry about that, Wicksy. I was, anyway.'

77

'Do you want to know how the story ends?'

Eddie shrugged. His hand was too shaky now to pick up his cup.

'The saga comes to a stop on Monday next, when I have to tell the goons I can't come up with any more cash. Not in the quantities they want. I reckon the least they'll do is kick bits off me until I'm not fit to walk. They're that kind of outfit, Eddie. I'm on a warning already. They've left me with no doubts. The future comes to a sharp stop three days from now.' Wicksy sat back in his chair. 'There's somethin' to tell the lads when you see them.'

'Christ, I'm sorry . . .'

'Prove it,' Wicksy said.

'What?'

'Show me how bad you feel. Put a few quid in my pocket so I can go on walkin' an' talkin' like a real human bein' until the next payment's due.'

'You know I'd help if I could,' Eddie said, his hands moving in agitated circles on the tablecloth. 'I'm in no position. I've got to think of myself *an*' Marie now. We've got plans – '

'An' plans cost money. Like mine did. The one you an' the others agreed to.'

'It wasn't our problem!' Eddie had shouted and he looked around now, as if somebody might come and throw him out. 'The problem was yours,' he said, quieter now. 'Hard but true. I'm sorry . . .'

'Sure, sure.' Wicksy nodded and went on nodding, his eyes still cold and unforgiving. 'It's been really somethin', seein' you again like this.'

Eddie pushed back his chair, stood, started to say something then turned and walked away. Wicksy, his face expressionless, picked up a paper napkin and wrapped his second doughnut in it.

Father Leary had been compared to a music-hall Irishman, the way he smoked a rustic pipe in the corner of his mouth, closed one eye when he listened to people and walked as if he was carrying something wide between his knees. He spoke like Barry Fitzgerald and wore a cassock stained with snuff, which he took when he couldn't smoke his pipe. He had been at St Martha's Catholic Church for eighteen years and would probably be there until he retired, some time in the late 1980s. That Friday afternoon, having conducted a funeral service and visited several sick parishioners in the local hospital, he took himself to the garden at the back of the church and sat on the bench against the west wall, puffing a pipeful of St Bruno.

He never thought of much when he took these little breaks, preferring to let his mind drift like the blue smoke trailing from the bowl of his pipe. He had been on the bench, arms folded, head back, for less than five minutes when he saw the young man wandering among the old tombstones at the foot of the garden.

Father Leary watched for a minute. The visitor had a detached look, walking slowly to no particular pattern, eyes on the ground. The gait, the stoop of the shoulders and the air of remoteness would have been natural in an older man; as it was, the priest decided he had a troubled soul on his hands.

'A fine afternoon for the time of year,' he called out.

Wicksy stopped, looking to see where the voice had come from. He spotted the old priest and nodded, approaching him.

'Thought I'd pop in an' have a look at the place,' he

said. 'I've passed it hundreds of times but I've never been inside. It's all right to walk here, is it?'

'Oh heavens yes.' Father Leary took the pipe from his mouth. 'I wish more people would. It's such a waste, me having it all to myself.' He patted the bench beside him. 'Sit down, if you've a mind to.'

'Cheers.'

Wicksy brushed his hand across the seasoned plank and sat beside the priest.

'I'm Jack Leary. You can call me Father or Jack, whichever suits you.'

'Simon Wicks.' They shook hands. 'You can call me Wicksy, like nearly everybody else does.'

'It's a pleasure to meet you, Wicksy. So what brings somebody so young on to the holy ground, apart from curiosity?' Father Leary's left eye narrowed, ready for the reply.

'Don't you get young people comin' about the church, then?'

'Not wanderin' about the grounds, no. There's the occasional older man or woman comes in from time to time, wonderin' about the place they'll be going before long. Churches start to fascinate people once they're past sixty. It's as if this is the vantage point where they can get a glimpse of what's beyond.'

'I can understand that,' Wicksy said.

'You didn't answer my question.'

'Sorry?'

'What brings you here?'

'Oh.' Wicksy shrugged. 'Just the curiosity, I suppose.' He looked at Father Leary, saw the mature lines of his face, the one eye wise and bright, the other half-shut and crafty. He could understand why people confessed to a man like this.

'And would there be maybe a shade of trouble?'

Wicksy smiled. 'It's that obvious, is it?'

'I'd say so. The troubled spirit's common enough to a man in my job. Easy to identify, even in a crowd. It's also common, for me at least, to pry into people's business. Is this trouble anything you can talk about?'

'It's nothin' anybody but myself could cure. An' I'm not in a position to do that.'

The priest drew on his pipe, making the tobacco glow and crackle. 'Talking about something and curing it aren't always the same. And you shouldn't ever believe there's no point in chatting about a problem if the chat won't sort it out. I don't happen to believe that a problem shared is a problem halved, but I do think there's some kind of ease to be got from getting the worry outside of yourself for a while, with words.'

'Yeah . . .'

Wicksy moved his feet back and forward on the gravel. Father Leary went on watching him. It was nearly a minute before Wicksy spoke.

'I'm in debt. Heavily. I'm not the only one in the world, I know that, but I'm in debt to some bad men. They do nasty things to people who get behind with the repayments. People like me.'

'And the time of your next repayment's close, is it?'

'Yes, it is.'

'And there's no hope of getting the money together?'

'None at all.'

The pipe crackled some more. Father Leary shifted on the bench, uncrossing and re-crossing his legs. Finally he took the pipe from his mouth and sighed.

'I should counsel you to pray. I take it that wouldn't appeal to you much?'

'I'm not really religious . . .'

81

'But I suspect you're an honest unbeliever, in which case the Lord'll forgive you, anyway. My second suggestion is that you should run. I'm not one to advocate that a person should welch on a debt, you understand, but this kind of debt – well, it's a lot different from owing money to a bank, isn't it? Bad men lending what's no doubt bad money don't deserve the ordinary decencies in their dealings with poor fallible souls. You should run, Wicksy.'

'I've thought about it . . .'

'But not too seriously,' Father Leary said. 'Pardon me for behaving like a mindreader, but you have a candid style about you – it tends to tell me a lot more than your words might.'

'I've even dreamed I ran away. But I don't know. It's hard to explain.'

The dream had been one of the rubber-legs variety, where Wicksy had made it out of Ilford and found himself in some strange part of the country, surrounded by old-fashioned buildings and a great many trees. He was away, but he had been followed. Men began to chase him down a leafy lane and when he tried to run his legs turned floppy and weak until finally he was crawling and they were closing on him, shouting and snarling. He woke up with a sheen of sweat, feeling breathless and very scared.

'Could the explanation be that you just don't like the idea of running out on anything?' Father Leary said.

Wicksy thought for a moment, then nodded. 'That's probably it. I never liked the idea of solvin' a problem by puttin' myself at a distance from it. An' there's another thing. Some people ran out on me, once. If I did somethin' like that it'd make me just like them.'

'I see your point. But if you're to be practical about this, I think you should look at the whole thing from a very down-to-earth angle and let your scruples go hang for the time being. A bruised conscience is a lot easier to live with than a broken back.'

'I suppose it is,' Wicksy said.

In silence they watched a sparrow perch on a tilting gravestone, peck at a patch of moss, then fly off.

'Now there's freedom for you,' the priest murmured. 'Our civilization's imprisoned us, hasn't it? We've built it and now we have to live up to it. If we don't, it crushes us.' He smiled, shaking his head slowly. 'I'm sorry – the last thing you need from me or anybody else is homespun philosophy.' He patted Wicksy's shoulder. 'I wish I could be some real help to you. In the old days you might have been offered sanctuary in the church. As things are nowadays, it's just as well the custom's died off. Sanctuary in the modern world would be a bit like taking a tranquillizer. It would only delay the showdown. Men who are owed money have long memories and they're good at keeping grudges alive.'

Wicksy stood up. 'Thanks for talking to me, Father.'

'It's the least anybody can do. Pity I couldn't have come up with an answer for you.'

'Maybe you did.'

Father Leary stood up slowly. 'Running away, you mean?'

Wicksy nodded. 'If I want a way out, that's it. Except I've been told I can't run away. The way they tell it, nowhere's far enough. They'd always find me.'

'Ah, well now,' Father Leary said, 'I know a thing or two about that kind of threat. It takes advantage of your deepest fears, the unreasonable ones. The Church has used the technique a lot in the past, I'm sorry to say. It keeps people toeing the line. Just think about it – how can a scruffy bunch of moneylenders keep track of a man who's determined to disappear? Men as determined as

83

that can outwit the resources of Scotland Yard, never mind a gang of hooligans whose only talent, a miserable one, is for cashing in on human need and weakness.'

'Yeah, you've got a point . . .'

'Of course I have, Wicksy.' Father Leary held out his hand. 'It's been good meeting you. Go away now and have a serious think about losing yourself.'

Wicksy got back to Pat's place in time to share a portion of fish and chips with her. She was quiet as they ate, appearing to watch the television but really, Wicksy noticed, looking just beyond the set, her eyes unfocussed and distant.

'Anythin' up?' he asked eventually.

'Nothin' you can help with.' Pat seemed to regret the coldness of the remark as soon as she had issued it. 'Sorry. I didn't mean to snap. I've had a rotten day an' it's got to me.'

'So what's wrong?' Wicksy recalled the priest's remark about talking being a good way to get a problem on the outside for a while. 'Even if I can't solve anythin', it might be a help to chat.'

'Maybe.' Pat pushed her plate away. 'They're goin' to take this place away from me. That's the whole top an' bottom of it.'

'You've been down that road more than once,' Wicksy said. 'You've always managed to sort somethin' out.'

'Not this time. They've got me stitched up tight.'

'Why do they want you out?'

'Oh, this an' that . . .'

'Rent, you mean?'

Pat nodded, staring at her cooling dinner.

'You mean you've let it slip back again? God, Mum, you know all you've got to do is stay up to date with the rent an' they leave you alone.'

'It's easy to preach. Help's what I need, not a lecture on managin' my affairs. I've got to get out. They reckon I've got three months at the most. An' even then I'll have to pay the back rent. Christ, what a world.'

All at once, angry as he was with Pat, Wicksy felt deflated. They were both in the same boat, after all. The separate outcomes might be different, were bound to be, but they stood on identical brinks for identical reasons. It hadn't occurred to Wicksy before that he might be a helpless product of genetics, powerless to stay out of trouble because of the imprint his mother had given him at conception. The idea seemed terribly feasible, now.

He stared at Pat, wondering if he should do what she was bound to do eventually – cut and run, vanish. The old priest had strongly recommended it and now Wicksy's instincts were getting keener on the idea. He had two days. Some time between now and sun-up on Monday he would have to run, if he wanted to avoid the sure alternative.

Run, his blood began to sing. *Run!* The priest was right, they would never find him if he ran fast enough and far enough. *Run!* But where?

Saturday

The instant she walked into the Thornton's lounge Pat decided her luck was going to change. She had read somewhere – and believed it strongly – that fortune travelled in currents of good and bad; people were drawn into one or the other depending on their vibrations at a given time each week. The given time, in Pat's case, was usually a Saturday when she went out to meet up with some of her friends for a lunchtime drink. She knew, with profound conviction, that whatever kind of luck she attracted on a Saturday, it would stick with her until the same time next week, when her governing vibrations would again decide how the following seven days would go.

The way the tall man at the bar looked at her she just knew she was giving off the right aura. Today, for the first time in ages, she had the vibes that would pull her into the good-luck current.

And there was something else. The man wasn't just another tall, so-so looking character who'd be pleased to spend a few pounds buying drinks for her. He was one of the dream kind, he was quality. His hair was iron-grey and clipped short; his square chin and firm mouth were a precise match for his dominantly angled nose and the mesmeric steadiness of his eyes. He wore an open black raincoat and under it a dark blue wool suit. His shirt looked like heavy white broadcloth and his blue tie was undoubtedly silk. The dream kind didn't often get into the Thornton. Pat's vibes, she decided, were at their throbbing best.

Diane, an old friend she hadn't seen for months, was sitting alone at a table near the corner of the bar. She waved to Pat, providing her with a perfect opportunity to glide past the big stranger, giving him a slow burn with half-lidded eyes. His expression didn't change, but she could tell he was interested.

'Well you're a sight for sore eyes,' Diane said, standing to put a wet kiss on Pat's cheek. 'What'll you have?'

'I'll get these,' Pat said. She glanced quickly and saw the man was watching. Pat felt a little shiver. She loved being watched by men of that kind. She was sure they caught something special in her, the sensual shimmer other men missed. 'You'll have a vodka an' tonic as usual, right?'

'Right.'

At the bar Pat stood about six feet from the man. She pretended to look round the room, as if she expected to see someone else she knew. The place was busy but it might as well have been a deserted oasis, with only that one figure leaning on the bar, holding his scotch glass. He dominated the room without moving a muscle.

'How've you been, Pat?' The barman, Archie, gave her the customary welcome of his gap-toothed grin.

'Not so bad.'

'Had an accident, have you?'

Pat frowned at Archie. 'How do you mean?'

'Your face. That's a nasty-looking bruise.'

Damn! she thought. She had put on a lot of foundation and in the gloomy light of the bathroom it had seemed to cover the mark perfectly. She hadn't allowed for the strong light in the Thornton. What would the big chap think of the mark? Would he even care? There was a lot of interest in his eyes, calm and controlled but still intense, in an odd way. Pat decided the bruise didn't obstruct whatever drew his attention to her.

'I bumped it on the corner of a cupboard in the kitchen,' she told Archie.

'I keep tellin' you,' he said, 'you should take more water with it.' Cackling, he reached for a glass. 'Usual?'

'Please. An' a vodka an' tonic.'

She wondered if the man would make a move. They didn't always. Sometimes they just stared for a while, then she'd look round and they'd be gone. The trouble was, she suspected, that she didn't always offer enough encouragement, or if the man was on the shy side she'd occasionally offer too much and scare him off. As she took the drinks and went back to the table she risked a tiny smile in his direction. She was sure his lips twitched in response.

'Right,' Diane said, taking her drink as Pat sat down. 'Give me all the dirt. I've a lot of gossip to catch up on.'

'Where have you been, anyway?' Pat puckered her brows with overdone interest. She had taken a chair where she could see the man by turning her head only a fraction, and he could look at her without seeing the bruise. 'I began to think you'd moved out of the district.'

'I've been in hospital,' Diane said, then lowering her voice she added, 'I've had the lot taken away.'

'Oh, dear . . .' Pat shook her head pityingly, thinking how much more, as the years passed, Diane resembled a Pekinese. 'I keep hearin' about women I know havin' that op. It's our age, I suppose. As time passes the complications build up, don't they?'

Time the enemy, time the thief . . . Pat read the line when she was a schoolgirl. It had stuck in her mind and in recent years she had come to understand its severe truth. There were times when she scarcely felt female, let alone feminine. But she could still turn the occasional head, and that was what counted. Use it while you've got it, that was her motto.

She glanced at the man again. He was still watching, and he was holding a fresh drink now. There was hope.

'It took me weeks to get over it,' Diane said. 'But the doctors told me I'll feel like a new woman, in time.'

'Maybe I should have it done, then.'

Pat could keep her side of the conversation going on automatic pilot for as long as she needed to. The drill was to keep letting the man know she was interested and encouraging him to interrupt on some pretext. To make an approach herself would be wrong with somebody like him. He would think she was cheap.

'I met this marvellous woman when I was in hospital,' Diane said, then launched into the story of how she had thought the poor dear was dying, she looked so ill lying in the next bed. But it had been the operation, the hysterectomy, that had made her look so bad, and in time she was able to help Diane through her own post-operative problems. They had become sound friends. 'I'm meetin' her after I leave here. We're goin' to the pictures. She's a great one for Saturday afternoon pictures.' Diane looked at the clock. 'I better drink up, come to think of it. I said I'd meet her at half-past one an' it's quarter past already. It'll take me ten minutes to get there. I'll leave you a drink behind the bar before I go, Pat.'

'Don't worry about that,' Pat said. 'Get me one next time.'

Five minutes, Pat thought. In terms of pub-pickup time that set a hopeless deadline. Sometimes the eye-manoeuvring could go on for half an hour and more. She hoped some of her mates would come in before Diane left; she didn't want to sit on her own, because that always hinted at the likelihood of a woman being on the game – a probability that would drive Mr Dreamboat away for certain.

After Diane had been given a summary of events that

occurred in her absence, she stood to drain her glass, told Pat she would be in touch, and left. The door was still swinging after her when the man solved the problem of contact by coming directly to the table and asking Pat if she minded him joining her. Naturally she didn't and said so, but she was surprised; the approach was more straight-line and swift than she expected from his type.

'I know this is going to sound like a very corny line,' he said, drawing the chair closer to Pat's, 'but I'm sure I know you, or at least I've met you somewhere.'

Pat observed two things. Up close there was a danger-ous look about the man, hard to define but somehow connected with the way he used his eyes. And he was a Scot.

'Oh, I've worked here an' there in the district for years,' Pat said. She puckered her mouth and made a smile of it, her usual concession to modest behaviour when she first spoke to a man. 'I can't say I know your face, mind you.'

'I could have sworn we'd met – still.' The man spread his hands on the table, palm up, a kind of apology. 'I'm always making mistakes like that. My name's Ian, by the way.'

'Pat. Nice to meet you, Ian.'

'My pleasure. And what's yours?'

'Pardon?'

'Your pleasure.' He pointed to Pat's glass. 'What'll you have to drink?'

'Oh. Well, in here I drink whisky, thanks.'

He was gone to the bar and back again, bearing two scotches, in less than a minute. Pat noticed the barman had served him straight away, even though the area round the bar was getting busy. He had command about him, she thought. Barmen saw him at once and he didn't have to wave his arms or shout to get attention. He had real presence. She liked that in a man.

'So.' Ian put his new drink alongside the other, which was only one-third gone. 'Tell me about yourself, Pat.'

'Oh, there's not a lot to tell.' Pat shrugged, laying on a touch of self-deprecation. 'I work part-time in a pub, an' when I'm not doin' that I look after my home. Dull stuff, really.'

'I wouldn't say you're dull at all. A married woman, are you?'

'I was. Not any more.'

'That's a shame.'

'No it isn't. As I see it, I'm better off the way I am. I'm not tied, I'm free. Do what I like when I like.'

'Ah can see that side to it,' Ian said. 'But there's always something kind of sad about a woman on her own. It never seems natural to me. A woman needs to be protected, and that's a man's job.'

'As long as it's the right man,' Pat said while in her head she was saying, 'God and wouldn't you be just the right man, wouldn't you just!'

'Oh yes, a good match is important. Very important.' Ian's eyes probed Pat's for a moment. 'Do you have kids, at all?'

'Two,' she said, knowing that it was always best to tell the truth in the matter of offspring. They had an embarrassing habit of turning up ten minutes after their existence had been denied. 'Both boys, both pretty-well grown up now. I was married young,' she added hastily.

'Are they good attentive sons? I mean do they look after you?'

'Not really. But I don't hold that against them. Kids have to be given their freedom.'

'But a boy should never turn his back on his mother.' There was a presbyterian finality about the way Ian said that. 'A father disciplines his sons, but it's their mother that makes them the men they are.'

'That's very true,' Pat sighed. 'I'll bet you were good to your mum.'

'I still go and see her in Glasgow, twice a year. She's old and frail and can hardly see, but she's still my mother. She's the woman that made me what I am.'

'What are you exactly?' Pat asked, hoping she hadn't shown indecent haste to find out his status. 'I mean what is it you do?'

'I'm in finance,' Ian said curtly.

Jackpot! He was in *finance*! Money was his business! And the way he looked at her, the interest he showed, it was unmistakable. Pat swallowed sharply.

'That sounds like an interesting job.'

'There are worse ones.' Ian sat back to sip his drink. He savoured the scotch on his tongue for a moment and swallowed it. 'So you don't see your sons, eh? That's a shame.'

Pat was more interested in talking about Ian's job and finding out if he was tied in any way, but she wasn't about to push the conversation in any direction he didn't want it to go.

'One of them's livin' with me at the moment,' she said. 'Livin' off me's a more accurate way of puttin' it, I suppose. But a mum can't deny her kids, right?'

'What's his name?'

'Simon.'

Pat saw a transformation. Ian sat up in his chair, his face tightening in the manner of a man who has solved a problem and sees an immediate way forward.

'Where abouts do you live, Pat?'

'Dover Road,' she said. 'Number fifty-seven.' Why was he asking? And why had his tone changed? 'I've been there quite a while, now.'

Now Ian sat back, held his glass between both hands and looked at it. Pat sipped her drink, watching him. He didn't seem the dream kind now; she felt she was in the presence of someone in authority, someone with an unpleasant message for her, like the man from the council.

'Do you live round here?' she asked, to shift the wedge of silence between them.

Ian looked up. 'Near here,' he said. He swallowed the remaining whisky in his glass, picked up the other one and drank half of that. He let out his breath slowly. 'I have to get going, Mrs Wicks. Saturday's a busy day for me.'

Pat watched him gulp down the rest of his drink.

'How did you know my name was Wicks?'

'Oh, I've known your name for a long time. I knew you'd be in here today. You're here just about every Saturday afternoon. A creature of habit, as they say.' Ian smiled, his lips moving stiffly as if they didn't do that very often.

'How come you needed to know my name?' Pat felt she had been intruded upon, and that feeling was tangled with a sense of rejection. She took in the change in the man, the businesslike way he was buttoning his jacket and making ready to leave. 'What did you buy me a drink for?'

'It was a civilized thing to do.' Again Ian smiled, as stiffly as before. He stood and pushed back his chair. 'It was nice meeting you,' he said.

'Just what's your game?' Suspicion and resentment were to the fore now as Pat stared up at the tall Scot.

'I'm not a game player, Mrs Wicks.'

'I don't use that name now, for your information.'

Ian shrugged, buttoning his raincoat. 'What's in a name, eh?'

The removal of bright expectation had made Pat irritably aware that her vibes, today, were no better than they had been for weeks. Whatever this man was, he wasn't any kind of good fortune. A warning bell rang in her memory and she stood up, hands gripping the table.

'Why did you want to know about my son? As soon as I told you about him you went all different.'

'It's business,' Ian said. 'Just business. You're easier to keep tabs on than your Simon is. I wouldn't have bothered you if I hadn't thought it was necessary.' He nodded sharply, a farewell, then turned and left.

Less than five minutes later Pat was in the public bar at the Ginger Giant. She stood at the end of the bar and waited until Wicksy had finished serving a customer, then she told him what had happened in the Thornton.

'What the hell's it all about, Simon?'

Wicksy stared at the etched-glass window behind Pat.

'Well?' Pat urged.

'You told him I was staying with you?'

'Yes, I did.'

'That's what he wanted to know, then,' Wicksy said.

'But why? Who is he?'

'He's part of my problem. An' now he knows where I live.'

'Jesus,' Pat breathed. 'All the troubles I've got, an' now you give me more.'

'Me?' Wicksy glared at her. 'It was you that did all the talkin' to the guy.'

'He bloody-well conned me! If you hadn't been involved with him he wouldn't have come near!'

'Don't shout,' Wicksy hissed. 'I'm tryin' to hold down a job here.'

'Sod your job!' Pat's mind was racing. The implications were building up. 'For the precious little time I've got a roof over my head, I'm goin' to get terrorized by hoodlums at the door. That's what it'll come to. Admit it – it's that bad, isn't it? You're in worse trouble than you ever told me. By the look of that Jock he could pull somebody's ears off without breakin' sweat. He's got a dangerous look about him . . .'

'It's me they want, not you. An' they don't exactly want to do anythin' to me yet. Not quite yet.'

Pat thumped her fist on the bar. 'They'll use me to get at you if it suits them! I've heard about these things!' She grasped Wicksy's wrist. 'I want you out! You can't stay at the house any more!'

'What?' Wicksy couldn't believe she meant it. 'You're chuckin' me out on the street?'

'Same thing as'll happen to me in a couple of months or so. But at least I'll be able to sleep if I know you're not in the place an' there's no goons hangin' about outside.'

'Thanks a lot,' Wicksy said.

'I'm only bein' practical. I'm protectin' myself, since there's nobody else to do it for me.' Pat stepped back from the bar. 'As soon as you finish here today I want you to come straight round the house, pack your stuff an' go. I mean it, Simon.'

'Where'll I go *to*?'

'You've found places before. I daresay you can do it again.'

'Yeah. Sure. It'll be a doddle,' Wicksy said, wondering how much more could happen before the big, final crunch.

There had been a time when music was everything. It had filled his days and invaded his sleep. He read nothing but music papers and pop biographies. The limited experience of his life was dredged and sifted to make material for lyrics, and he could distil tunes from the discord of traffic noises. That had been the magic time, a period of innocent obsession that was gone forever. Now he couldn't even think of a single tune to distract himself.

That afternoon had been full of indecision and aborted impulses. He had left his two bags at the pub with Jacko – he told him it was some spare gear he was giving a friend later – and then started walking wondering what to do. He couldn't think of anybody who would put him up. If he asked Jacko there would be quizzing and fretting and finally, for sure, a regretful refusal, because Jacko wanted no disturbance in his dull, solitary, safe life.

Wicksy wandered for a couple of hours, keeping off the main streets, hoping he might see somebody he knew well enough to put the arm on, anybody at all who could let him have a space to sleep in. Halfway through his aimless criss-crossing of Ilford he suddenly thought of the car and was clutched with panic. If the sharks saw it parked on the open lot near his mother's house they might take it. They were bound to know it was his. They knew everything. Wicksy went back to the lot, drove the car half a mile to a row of derelict under-the-arches lockups and parked it behind a big mound of rubble.

Switching off the engine, he asked himself why he wasn't running. He had every reason. If he went now he would have a good start; the longer he delayed the shorter his lead would be. Yet he had been delaying and he knew it was deliberate, without examining his reason. Until now.

It wasn't scruples. The priest had been right – a sore conscience was preferable to a divided spine. And it wasn't because Wicksy couldn't think of anywhere to go. That would sort itself out, he'd decided, if he simply switched on the engine again and took off. He sat back in the bucket seat and closed his eyes, trying to give a shape to whatever impulse kept him hanging around Ilford.

It came to him. He wouldn't run because it would close a door. He hated closing doors. Some people called it burning boats, but to Wicksy any action that prevented him from changing his mind, or from relenting, was the closing of a door. A self-locking door. So far he had been passive in his dealings with the loan sharks. He had done nothing active to offend them – failure to pay wasn't the same thing as refusal. To run would be an active gesture which would cause incurable offence. They would be after him. Always.

He sat forward, put his elbows on the steering wheel and told himself that was rubbish. Sooner or later they would get fed up looking for him.

'Of course they would,' he whispered, putting conviction behind the words.

But it still sounded hollow. He couldn't make himself believe it. His unreasonable fears had been activated, just as Father Leary had said. Unreasonable or not, they were fears, terrible ones. If he ran away he would never feel safe again.

He got out of the car, locked it and walked half a mile to a street where there was a small museum of pre-war British cinema. It was run by Geoff Ridges, a man who lived for movies that had been made long before he was born. He had opened the museum with a legacy from his grandfather and filled it from a garage crammed with the collection of memorabilia he had built, adoringly, for twenty years.

Geoff was thirty-five and although he wasn't in Wicksy's age group and they had no interests in common, they had always got along well together. The first time they met was at an Arts Week gathering, arranged by the council as a gesture of thanks to people who had helped. Wicksy had played piano at a couple of official dances and Geoff had delivered a lecture on the work of Sir Alexander Korda. Each liked the other, Wicksy guessed, because of the one thing they had in common at that time – intense enthusiasm for what they did.

The museum was three connecting sixteen-by-sixteen rooms, brightly striplighted, containing rows of stands and clusters of glass cases displaying photographs, props and costumes from more than two hundred productions. There were frames on the walls containing original set plans and production schedules; in the farthest room a video machine ran taped copies of classics from the 'thirties on a huge black-and-white monitor. Visitors could buy postcard reproductions of studio stills and old posters.

But there were never many visitors. Other buffs would drop in occasionally to swap lore with Geoff, and an occasional curious passer-by would pay his fifty pence and fail to stay for long. Today, while conventional enterprises had been enjoying a decent weekend trade, only three visitors had set foot in the museum. Geoff didn't seem upset by that. Without ever saying so, he gave the impression that he had opened this shrine for his own pleasure. If other people cared to share in it from time to time that was fine, but it wasn't essential.

'I was just going to shut up shop.' Geoff, with fright-wig hair and granny specs, led Wicksy into his little office, its walls covered with movie stills and magazine clippings. 'I'm glad you came. We can use up this milk in our coffee, instead of me forgetting to take it home and coming back to the stink of it on Monday morning.' He pulled a chair out from the front of his chipped plywood desk and removed a bundle of magazines from the seat. 'Park yourself.'

'Ta.' Wicksy sat down. 'You're sure you don't want to get off home? I didn't realize how late it was getting.'

'If it wasn't for the fact I've got my dad and a budgie back at the house, I think I'd move in here,' Geoff said.

'Time doesn't mean much anyway, not when you live in the past. Which,' he added, switching on the kettle by the wall, 'is a bloody sight better place to inhabit than the present.'

'I'll go along with that,' Wicksy said.

'What brings you, anyway? A sudden attack of movie mania?'

'I think I fancied seein' a friendly face.'

Geoff rinsed two mugs at the miniature handbasin. He dried them, spooned in coffee powder and sugar, then leaned against the wall with his hands in his pockets, watching the kettle.

'Trouble?' he said after a minute. He was always cautious of prying. 'You look dejected. Chopfallen.'

'It's a long story. A borin' one, too. The bottom line is, I'm down on my luck an' out on the street.' Wicksy tapped the knuckle of his forefinger on the edge of the desk for a moment. 'I'll tell you the truth – I came over here on the off chance you could maybe put me up. Only for a few nights, until I can get myself sorted out.' Before Geoff spoke Wicksy put up his hand. 'If you can't accommodate me I'll understand. I know I'm imposin'.'

'No problem,' Geoff said.

'You mean it? You're not just sayin' that to be nice? I don't want to make any ripples for anybody . . .'

'No problem at all,' Geoff assured him, then said, 'Well, *one* problem. Dad.'

'He don't like visitors, the kind that stay the night?'

'No, nothing like that. Just the opposite in fact. The poor old bugger gets lonely in the evenings, now he hasn't got Mum to bicker with any more. The trouble is, he's into the Spanish Civil War. I mean really into it. He was there, you see. Now he's a sort of unofficial historian of the whole shooting match. He's read everything there is

99

on the topic and when he starts talking about it – well, you'll see what I mean.'

'I'll enjoy it,' Wicksy said, meaning what he said. Enthusiasts like Geoff and his father were the kind of people he should have cultivated long ago, instead of wandering into the company of pop people and getting himself in the mess he was in now. 'One of these days I'm goin' to be an expert on somethin' – maybe survival, if I'm lucky.'

Geoff asked for no details of Wicksy's trouble or how he got into it in the first place. Instead, as they drank their coffee, he talked about a consignment of silent-film goodies he had at home, waiting to be unpacked.

'It's a collection that was put together by a chap up in Lancashire. He died a month ago and his widow accepted my bid for the lot. There are prop guns, swords, helmets, paste jewellery, special-effects gear, old shooting scripts – it's an Aladdin's cave job.'

Wicksy listened, noticing again the burning enthusiasm, a commitment and fascination that would keep Geoff a happy man until the day he died. Through all his personal misery, Wicksy felt a pang of genuine envy. If only his childhood had been different, he thought. Or if he'd tried harder, in spite of his childhood. He could have been like that, secure in a world of his own choosing, instead of the one that had been thrust on him.

When they had drained their cups Geoff wrote his home address on a slip of paper and gave it to Wicksy.

'Get your gear and come round any time you like. We're having a take-away curry for dinner. If you fancy any get there before half-past seven. Otherwise Dad'll eat the lot.'

Wicksy went back to where he had parked the car, picking his way carefully across the darkened waste ground. Darkness had never troubled him much, it had only been an absence of light. Now it felt like a thick, menacing presence. He let himself into the car quickly and drove round to the Ginger Giant.

'I'll take them bags off you now, Jacko,' he said, stepping up to the bar.

Jacko nodded, drying washing-up water from his hands. He put down the towel and instead of going through to the back, where he'd put the bags, he came along to where Wicksy was standing. He was frowning.

'Is there anythin' I should know about?' he asked.

'Like what?'

'You tell me. There was that bit of rattle between you an' your mum at dinner time, then two minutes after I'd opened tonight, this geezer comes in askin' for you.'

'What'd he look like?'

'Tall, grey-haired, Scotch accent. He had a mean kind of manner, if you know what I mean. Didn't look like he worked for no friendly society.'

'Oh, him,' Wicksy said, his stomach shifting. 'He's just an old friend of the family.'

'I didn't know your family had any friends left. You're sure it's got nothin' to do with whatever your old lady was goin' on about earlier? I don't want no bother round here. You know my policy.'

'There's no trouble, Jacko. Take my word for it. Now can I have the bags, please?'

Jacko wandered through to the back and brought the luggage.

'You can't blame me for takin' on a bit, Simon,' he said, hoisting the bags on to the bar. 'I mean, three things happen in the one day that just sort of naturally connect in my head – well, I'm bound to think there's trouble buzzin' close to you, ain't I?'

'Three things?' Wicksy said.

Jacko looked at him suspiciously. 'You mean you didn't

hear about your dad – your stepdad, that is?'

Wicksy shook his head. 'Honest. I've not heard a dickybird.'

'He got picked up by the law. In Dougan's, the book-ie's. What I heard was, he'd fiddled a slip or somethin'. Anyhow, he's been charged, apparently.'

So it wasn't all bad news, Wicksy thought as he left the pub. He had been worried, faintly, that Brian might carry out his threat to send along a friend to dish out some malice. Faint as it had been, the worry had been an unwelcome addition to the straws already straining the camel's back. The best thing about the news of Brian's arrest, though, was that Pat wouldn't be bothered by him for a while.

When he got to the car Wicksy was wondering why he felt so relieved for his mother, considering the way she had treated him. The same old reason, he supposed. He was sorry for the good woman trapped inside that nasty big lump.

Then, as he stuck the key in the door lock, all thought fled. A man had come forward from the shadows and was leaning with his hand on the roof of the car, right beside Wicksy.

'Good evening, Simon.'

Wicksy could only see the bulk, not the face. But it was obvious from the accent who the man was.

'Oh. Hello, Mr Bryce.' What else could he say?

'I was in the district, so I thought I'd look you up.' Bryce's head moved nearer. Stray light from the pub window glinted dully on his eyes, making them look darkly metallic. 'It's policy to send out reminders in advance . . .'

'Yeah, right. But there's no need.' Wicksy's mouth was drying. 'I'll be there at the meet, just as arranged.'

102

'That's good, Simon. Excellent. I'd hate to think you'd let us down.'

For a wild instant Wicksy thought, what the hell, tell him, get it over with right now. Take away the tension, grit the teeth and take what's coming instead of waiting for it. But the impulse died. Terror rejected it and begged Wicksy to play for time.

'I know I've had my troubles with the payments a couple of times, Mr Bryce. But I'm gettin' it all sorted out now.'

Bryce was silent for a moment, then he breathed out very slowly. 'You mean if I asked you for Monday's payment right this minute, you could put your hand in your pocket and give it to me?'

'Well no . . .'

'Oh, that's *not* what you're telling me, then . . .' The voice was murderously soft, the promise of razor-edged steel under velvet.

'Well I wouldn't carry that kind of money with me, like . . .'

'But you could go and get it for me? I mean we could get in this wee motor of yours, drive somewhere and pick it up?'

Wicksy swallowed, his dry tongue chafing on his palate. 'It wouldn't be as easy as that.' His imagination was locked. He couldn't home in on the right lie, the one that would get him off this hook – if it was a hook. 'I can't actually have it until Monday . . .'

'Oh, I get it,' Bryce said, so close to Wicksy now that his breath could be felt. 'It's in a bank, eh? You're getting the maximum interest on the deposit.'

No! Don't fall for it! Don't prove there's no money!

'I don't deal with banks, Mr Bryce. Or they don't deal with me. I explained that to Mr Benson right at the start, when he made the loan.' The imagination eased a fraction. A lie came. 'The cash is bein' brought to me. It's my own, mind you, but I didn't want to risk losin' any of it. I put it in safe keepin'.'

'Well, I certainly hope so, Simon. I mean, there'll be no room for excuses on Monday, you realize that? You made a deal, we kept our side of it and you have to keep yours. The penalty – ' Bryce cut himself off. 'Well, we won't go into that.'

'No need to worry about penalties,' Wicksy said, finding his voice hopelessly feeble. 'You can stand on me, Mr Bryce.'

'I hope I don't have to.' The laugh was short, no more than a rasp. 'Don't be late on Monday, Simon. We don't want the hassle of having to come and look for ye.' Bryce squeezed Wicksy's arm momentarily, a superficially friendly gesture that demonstrated the strength in the fingers. 'I'll be seeing you.'

Bryce was gone as swiftly and quietly as he had arrived. Wicksy stood by the car, trembling, not sure if he could drive. When he finally eased himself in behind the wheel his fear was formulating an idea. He sat staring out at the dark, considering it, letting it harden. It was something that might work. For the moment he wasn't sure, his nervous system was too far out of whack to allow him the power of judgement. He would sleep on it, he decided, grateful again that there would be a bed where he could do that.

When he arrived at Geoff's place he found a magnificently lived-in house, the sitting room filled with overstuffed chairs, side tables and stools piled with books and old gramophone records, a massive musical box on a stand under the window and on top of it a blue and white budgie in a green enamelled cage. There were pictures on all four walls, dozens of them – battle scenes, seascapes, wild birds and, on one huge canvas in an antique gilt frame, a fearsome painting of a bull walrus.

'Quite a place,' Wicksy said as Geoff led him through to the kitchen to meet his father.

'I've an aunt who calls it Hatter's Castle,' Geoff said. 'But we like it. It suits us.'

Geoff's father certainly suited the house. He had the same spilling-over-at-the-seams appearance, a large, well upholstered man with Einstein-like hair, a thick white moustache and incredibly pink skin. He had one hand in the pocket of his grey cardigan, the other in a half opened take-away container, his forefinger and thumb teasing off a chunk of curried chicken.

'Dad, downpedal on the primitive stuff, eh? Our guest's arrived.'

The old man popped the meat into his mouth, licked his fingers and turned, beaming at Wicksy. Wicksy smiled back, instantly charmed.

'I'm Desmond.'

'And I'm Simon, but I'm usually called Wicksy.'

They shook hands.

'Welcome to our fortress,' Desmond said. 'I understand you'll be staying for a short time. Which is splendid. We're getting too much like a couple of old maids, Geoffrey and myself. Our conversation needs freshening.' He waved a hand imperiously towards the door. 'Now if you would both like to go back into the sitting room, I'll put the food on plates and bring it through to the pair of you. There are still one or two things I'm not too decrepit to manage.'

Wicksy followed Geoff back to the sitting room, realizing that this was precisely what he needed. Sanctuary. A fortress. A time apart in a totally different environment with two magic members of a dying species, Civilized Eccentric Man. He would have time here to get his perspectives straight – and to think out his idea carefully to see if it showed any promise of saving his neck.

Sunday

Todd Rumbold had once been a middleweight boxer. He was a popular, flamboyant figure who had only twice lost a bout during his professional career. He won big purses and showed the kind of promise that excited promoters and regularly fed the newsmen with back-page copy. But the eternal hazards of the boxing life flawed young Rumbold. By the time he was twenty-eight he had begun to keep bad company – gamblers, whores, criminals – and his marriage collapsed when his wife discovered he was keeping another woman in a flat in Ealing. Drink entered the picture, he began running up dangerous debts and his boxing dates began to dwindle. By the time he was thirty, in 1965, Todd was washed up.

Now, at sixty, he was the owner and operator of a games arcade. From eleven each weekday morning until ten at night he presided over twenty popping, shrieking and blasting simulations of intergalactic war. There were no snooker or tennis games in Todd's arcade, no comic electronic chases or escape-the-spook scenarios. 'War's what they want,' Todd had once said, expressing his entire business strategy. 'Kids have a lot of aggression. They have to take it out on somethin'. I put guns an' lasers in their hands an' they can kill an' maim to their hearts' content. I'm keepin' mayhem off the streets,' he'd added, adorning himself with a social conscience.

Wicksy had known Todd for three years. Their first meeting hadn't been a cordial event: Todd had warned Wicksy about putting the boot into the base of a machine each time he lost out to the marauding Blisterons in their

106

gunships. 'It's strictly nuclear warfare on this machine, kid,' Todd had warned. 'Kickin' ain't allowed.'

Wicksy had taken the warning and never molested a machine again. In time he and Todd grew to like each other. Wicksy struck the older man as being several cuts above the riffraff who usually spent their money in his arcade; Wicksy discovered, by stages, that the older man's experiences of life had given him a richly stocked philosophy that another person could learn from.

At ten o'clock Wicksy found Todd where he'd expected, in the office alongside the arcade, doing his books. Since the time he'd been bankrupted in the 'sixties, Todd had sworn that nothing so devastating would ever happen to him again. He was a meticulous book-keeper and never allowed his double entries, in life or business, to get out of balance.

'Well then Simon.' Todd looked up as Wicksy stuck his head round the door. 'How's it goin'?'

'Fine, thanks.'

'Come in an' shut the door. The draught's goin' for me poinsettia.'

'Sure I'm not interruptin' you?'

'Of course you're interruptin' me.' Todd took off his glasses and put them on the desk. 'But I need a bit of interruptin', I think. I've been at this for more than an hour.'

He leaned back in his chair and stretched. Even now, half bald, his face lined and his eyes an old man's watery blue, he gave the impression of abundant physical power. His hands dropped to the desk as fists, formidably bulky and hard.

'Still workin' for Jacko?' he asked.

Wicksy nodded.

'Can't be a lot of laughs. Does that explain it?'

'Explain what?'

'The look you've got. Like a bloke tryin' to put on a cheerful face while they're leadin' him to the guillotine.'

'I can't hide anythin' from you, can I?'

'Yes you can,' Todd said. 'Anybody can hide anythin' from anybody, if they want to, or have to. You've got somethin' you don't want to hide from me, that's all.' Todd looked at the sunlight beyond the office's solitary window. 'Fancy takin' a stroll?'

Wicksy said he thought that was a good idea. Todd stood, closed his ledger and put it with the invoices and receipts in the desk drawer. He locked it, slipped on his heavy tweed jacket and wrapped a woolly blue scarf twice round his neck.

'Right,' he said. 'We'll take my old trainin' route – up Bromford Road, along Reeves Terrace an' twice round the park.'

The air outside was cool and fresh, with a tang of leaf mould from the gardens they passed. Todd's pace was brisk and measured; Wicksy took a couple of minutes to match it.

'Nothin' better than walkin',' Todd said as they turned the corner on to Reeves Terrace. 'It keeps the muscles goin' an' gets the blood movin' round the brain. It doesn't matter how bad you're feelin' about anythin', you'll always feel a bit better if you get out an' walk an' have a good think while you're doin' it.'

'Yeah, I suppose so,' Wicksy said.

Todd glanced at him. 'So what is it that's botherin' you?'

Wicksy told him. He never had any difficulty telling Todd anything, because he was a man who had done a lot of things in his life that were wrong and misguided, so he never moralized.

'Did you come to see me because you thought I could find an answer for you?'

'No,' Wicksy said. 'If I'd thought that I'd have talked to you long before now.'

'So you just came to see me because you fancied lookin' up an old acquaintance?' Again Todd glanced at Wicksy.

'I'm stoppin' with a mate just now,' Wicksy said. 'This mornin' I was talkin' to his dad. Great old bloke, he is. He knows all there is to know about the Spanish Civil War an' European history an' God knows what else. An' he's not borin' with it, he can really get a grip on your imagination when he talks to you. But somethin' started makin' me uncomfortable, after I'd been listenin' to him for a bit. The fix I'm in, see, the last thing I need is to get my head into this escapist bit. I mean I was dwellin' in past things with this old bloke, safe things. What I wanted, suddenly, was to talk to somebody that . . .' He paused, trying to find the right words.

'Somebody like me, that's had to meet nasty deadlines like the one you're facin',' Todd said. 'I know what you mean. I did time, once. Six months in the Scrubs. I knew it was goin' to happen, or I was just about sure. So before I knew it I was hangin' round with old lags, lappin' up their reminiscences, tryin' to convince myself that bad as prison might be, things would be all right in the end. These men were livin' proof.'

'Yeah,' Wicksy said. 'That's it, I suppose.'

They walked on in silence for a minute.

'You definitely can't raise the money?' Todd said as they walked through the park gates.

'Not a chance. An' even if I could, I'd have to find the dosh for the next payment, an' the next.'

'An' you've got no contingency plan?'

'One,' Wicksy said. 'I still can't make up my mind if I could swing it, though.'

'Let me hear it.'

Wicksy explained what he had worked out. When he

109

was finished Todd was walking with his eyes down, staring at the path.

'What do you think?' Wicksy asked him.

'It's a bit hairy. It could work, mind you. Or it could go so bad you'd wish to Christ you'd never tried it.'

'That's what I've been thinkin'.'

They passed a bunch of small boys kicking a ball around on the grass.

'It'd be nice to be that age again, eh Simon? Not a care, everythin' up ahead of you. I reckon if we knew at their age what we learn about the world later, we'd just go on kickin' a ball about till we snuffed it.'

'Tell me somethin',' Wicksy said when they were half-way round the park. 'If I put it to them honest, Benson an' his lads, just tell them plain, with no excuses, that I can't meet the payments – is there maybe a chance they'd let up on me?'

'There's more chance of Maggie Thatcher defectin' to Russia,' Todd said. He gave Wicksy a glum look. 'When I fell down on my instalments back in the 'sixties, I levelled with the people I owed. Told them the plain, sad truth. An' they put me in hospital for eight weeks.' He watched Wicksy's reaction. 'I'm not sayin' all this to scare you. I wouldn't do that. But I'm not goin' to build up useless hopes for you, either. You say you've got a bad feelin' about doin' a runner, but that's what you should do. Piss off, fast.'

'There was even a priest told me to do that.'

'An' he was right. I wished I'd done it. I've got healed fractures that hurt so bad some days, I still wish I'd done it.'

'Sometimes I think it's a dream,' Wicksy said. 'Wide awake, worryin' my guts out, I suddenly get the feelin' it's not happenin' at all. For minutes on end I'm positive

110

that nothin' this bad *couldn't* happen to me. Then I get the other feelin', that I'm goin' off my head.'

'You won't do that. I know the kind that go barmy an' you're not one of them. But one thing I'll warn you – you could turn very weird in here.' Todd touched his heart. 'I've seen that happen. A man can get so much sufferin' he never deserved, with no compensation at the end of it, that he turns on himself. It's possible to hate yourself, Simon. To hate yourself for what you've brought on yourself. Don't let that happen. Keep rememberin' that none of this is really your fault. You got in trouble because your hopes outweighed your chances an' your mates were no kind of mates at all. There's nothin' there to punish yourself for.'

They slowed down as an old tramp approached, his hand outstretched. Todd dug in his pocket and gave him the forty pence he found there.

'Poor bastard,' he murmured as they moved on. 'I used to be scared I'd end up like that. Maybe I still am.'

Wicksy sniffed. 'I'd settle for windin' up like him if it'd get me off the spike.'

'That's daft,' Todd said. 'What you're sayin' is, you'd settle for no hope at all, instead of the bit of hope you've got.'

'You reckon I've some hope, then?'

'Sure. If you bugger off, smartish.'

'I told you what I think about that.'

'Even so,' Todd grunted. 'I know loan sharks are good at locatin' runaways, but I'm sure they don't catch up with them all. Get away from the London area, right out into the country. Or go up north.'

'That wouldn't work. Don't ask me why, I just know I'd get so low, away from the old Smoke, that I wouldn't make a go of anythin'. I'd get homesick, even though I've got no home.'

111

'Well, run *some*where. Don't kid yourself that these men you've been dealin' with'll ever get infected with charity. An' one other thing – don't imagine you know what real pain is. I thought I did, until I had a professional job done on me.'

When the walk was over and they were standing outside the shuttered arcade again, Todd put a hand on Wicksy's shoulder and squeezed it.

'I know you thought it would help, comin' an' talkin' to me. But I've done you no good, son. The fact is, nobody will. It's all down to yourself. That's the only advice I've got – trust yourself, an' as few other people as you have to.'

'Thanks for the walk, anyway,' Wicksy said. 'I'll be seein' you, Todd.'

'Well, if you do come an' see me again, remember I want you to be fit enough to do a couple of circuits of the park with me. Remember my advice . . .'

'Yeah,' Wicksy said. 'I know. Run.'

Sunday felt like a one-day amnesty. All bets and penalties were suspended. The streets were empty, there was hardly any traffic and the relative quiet was like a soothing reminder that even bad men put their feet up on the sabbath.

One man who did have business that day was loitering near the corner door of the Ginger Giant, trying to look normal. Which was difficult for him, even when he was in a crowd. He was Terence Hill, thirty-five, a tall man with cagey eyes and a grotesquely misaligned hare lip. People found themselves staring at it, when they weren't staring at the place where his left ear should have been. All Terence had there was a knob of gristle the size of a marble. He had lost the ear in childhood, when a car knocked him off his bicycle and left him sitting in the gutter, stunned, feeling warm blood on his neck and seeing a puzzling pink object lying in the road, at just the spot where his head had made momentary, glancing contact. The surgeon had botched his efforts at replacing the ear, and later at rebuilding it, just as years before another man had failed to align properly the two sides of Terence's malformed upper lip.

He had deliberately arrived at the Ginger Giant before it opened, so he would be in the alley at the side of the pub when Wicksy came that way to begin his lunchtime stint. The alley was shaded from the sun and a cold breeze blew up from the main road, making Terence uncomfortable and turning the scar tissue on his lip purple. On the other hand the cold made him resent Wicksy, and an edge of resentment helped on a job like this.

At ten to twelve, as Terence was rubbing his hands and stamping his feet to boost his circulation, Wicksy appeared at the bottom of the alley. He had his head down and his hands buried in the pockets of his bomber jacket.

'Right,' Terence breathed, moving towards his target.

Wicksy glanced up when the strange-looking man was about three yards away. He caught the malicious intent and tried to jump aside. Terence went at him with outstretched arms, grabbing the shoulders of his jacket.

'This is a message pal, from you-know-who!'

Wicksy's breath caught with terror as one hand left his shoulder, bunched and came swinging at his head. He ducked and felt the man go off-balance. Without thinking he brought up his own right fist and connected, hitting the man at the soft angle of his neck and chin. He gulped and Wicksy punched him again, this time in the stomach. The cobbles of the alley gave hardly any purchase to thin-soled shoes and after a moment's groaning and teetering, during which time Wicksy punched him again, the assailant tried to run clear, slipped and landed on his back.

Wicksy looked down at him, puzzled. Was that it? Was that what he'd been worrying himself about? The man on the ground looked evil enough, but he was a pussycat. He hadn't the first idea about how to initiate an assault and he had no aim at all. And he was dead easy to thump. Wicksy took a step nearer and Terence put up a hand, wheezing loudly as he tried to breathe.

'No . . . No, don't . . .'

Totally baffled now, Wicksy reached down, pulled the man to his feet and leaned him on the wall.

'It's all right, mate,' Terence burbled, shielding his face. 'No need, you've made your point . . .'

'What's all this about?' It was dawning on Wicksy that Benson hadn't, as yet, any reason to set the heavies on him. If this could be called a heavy. 'What'd you try to jump me for?'

'I was sent to,' Terence said, rubbing his outraged stomach. 'You were a job . . .'

'Somebody sent you to duff me up?'

'Yeah, that's it. Nothin' personal an' I cocked it up anyway. Let's just forget it, eh?'

'But who sent you?'

'I can't say.'

'You better say,' Wicksy muttered, 'or you'll cop for some more. I'm not even breathin' hard yet.'

'Brian Wicks,' Terence yelped. 'He showed me your picture, told me where you worked an' paid me to do the business.'

If he hadn't been so unbalanced by the suddenness of what happened Wicksy would have laughed. He stood back from Terence, staring at him.

'Brian Wicks sent *you* to work me over? Jesus, he never changes, does he? Always does things on the cheap. How much did he give you?'

Terence ran his tongue along his deformed lip. 'Well, he didn't actually let me have it. It was to be payment after the job was done.'

'How much?'

'A fiver.'

Wicksy had never heard of a five-pound contract being taken out on anybody.

'Is that your usual rate?'

'Brian's a bit of a mate . . .'

'That figures. Have you done much of this kind of thing?'

Terence was getting back his composure. He dusted his jacket and slapped the knees of his trousers.

'Don't think I'm not up to it,' he said.

'Oh yeah, I'm sure you can be a killer on your good days.'

'I've done a few jobs for bookies an' such.'

Wicksy nodded. 'Old guys, cripples, blind men . . .'

Terence put on a warning look, which was a mistake. Wicksy slapped him on the face. Terence cringed.

'I ought to kick skittles out of you, hit man. But in the circumstances, what with you not gettin' paid an' makin' a pratt of yourself into the bargain, I'll let it go.' Wicksy paused and began to smile, without having to force it. 'You realize you wouldn't have got paid even if your mission had worked out?'

'How's that?'

'Brian's been nicked. Yesterday, it was. He tried to put one over in a bettin' shop – maybe the bookie'll hire you to sort him out when the law's finished with him.'

Terence moved cautiously away from the wall.

'Tell us somethin',' he said, eyeing the lower end of the alley, getting ready to take off. 'What's Brian got against you, anyway?'

'I'm his stepson. He can't forgive me for not turnin' out to be the kind of lad he wanted me to be.'

Terence said nothing. Wicksy turned and walked away.

The lunchtime trade in the Ginger Giant was brisk, but the atmosphere wasn't as cheerful as usual. The night before one of the oldest and most regular punters had died. His drinking mate sat wan and silent in a corner while men reminisced and sighed over their pints. As a mark of respect Jacko kept the dartboard light switched off and issued no playing cards, crib boards or boxes of dominoes.

'My back's played me up chronic all night,' he confided to Wicksy. 'I've had hardly any sleep. I was just thinkin', while I was makin' a cup of tea at seven this mornin', I should have a holiday. Go abroad, maybe.'

'But you've never done that,' Wicksy pointed out.

It was true. In all his life Jacko had been on holiday only once, when he was a boy of twelve. He had never been out of England and had never expressed a wish, until now, to be anywhere but Ilford.

'Oh, I'm gettin' restless. I feel shut in. I watch the telly sometimes an' see them beaches in Spain, all that sun an' the blue sea, an' I get a definite hankerin' to lap up some of it.' Jacko gazed wistfully at the patch of greying sky beyond the window. 'To tell you the truth, Simon, I wouldn't mind just disappearin' – you know, goin' to a new place with a new name, a different identity. I'm fed up bein' me.'

It was a rare moment of candour and it struck Wicksy the more forcibly because Jacko was echoing his own dearest wish, to become another person, to be *anybody* but Simon Wicks.

'I knew a bloke once who did it,' Jacko went on. 'Came from round here, he did. He was married to an old boot that gave him twenty-odd years of misery. He was in a lousy job an' his kids were nothin' but trouble to him. So one day he said to himself, sod it, I've had enough of this. So he did a bit of plannin', an' he vanished.'

'You mean they never found him?'

'Never. An' it wasn't for the want of tryin'. His wife an' one of the sons spent more than two years tryin' to track him down. They even had a couple of private eyes on the job at one point, but they didn't have any luck.'

'Blimey.' Wicksy was intrigued. He stepped away from Jacko for a minute to serve a customer, then he came back. 'How d'you reckon the bloke did it, just disappearin' like that?'

'He was clever.'

'Left the country, maybe.'

'No, he didn't do that,' Jacko said, looking guarded now. 'Like I said, he was clever, that's all.'

'You know how he did it, do you?'

Jacko nodded. 'He told me. But I promised him I'd say nothin' to anybody else.'

Wicksy was frowning. 'He told you? You mean he came back?'

'Yes. Just once. He said he'd fancied comin' back an' walkin' past his house, slow an' easy, knowin' that even if his family saw him, he'd be ignored.'

'Ignored? How come?'

Jacko shrugged. 'I don't suppose it hurts, tellin' somebody about it, as long as I don't tell you his name.'

There was a sudden flurry of business and it was five minutes before Jacko could explain his friend's disappearing act.

'He moved less than five miles away. That was the first clever bit, because he knew they'd think he'd be in another part of the country. An' he'd planned things, like I told you. The plans were laid nearly two years before he actually went.'

117

'Two years?' Wicksy said. 'That's a hell of a long time to hang on, isn't it? Why did he wait so long?'

'He waited so that people, his family an' them that knew him, would get used to what he looked like.' Jacko chuckled softly. 'When he decided he was goin' to make the break, I mean when the idea first came to him, he began eatin' like a pig. In the space of three months he put on four stone. An' he kept it on. He was really fat. He grew a beard, too, a big bushy job. An' cleverest of all, he went bald.'

'How'd he do that?'

'With scissors an' a razor. He started recedin' at the front an' developed a bald spot on top. In no time at all the two met up an' all he was left with was a fringe, round the back of his head and above his ears. He told me later he'd had to get up an hour earlier in the mornin's to keep the baldness goin'.' Jacko shook his head admiringly. 'He really worked at it.'

'So what happened?' Wicksy asked, beginning to guess.

'When he left, he laid low for about six months. He put himself on a strict diet an' lost nearly five stone. He let his hair grow back an' he shaved off the beard.'

'Bloody hell – '

'With a moustache – he'd never had one in his life before – an' a pair of specs with plain glass in them, he was a new man. The description of him that was circulated didn't come anywhere near what he looked like any more. An' I swear to you, I didn't recognize him the day he came back an' walked in here. What I'd remembered was a big fat bald bloke, definitely a bit of a slob, with a beard. Now he was thin, clean chinned, with a healthy head of hair an' the look of a bank clerk about him. It was amazin'. He'd a hard job convincin' me it was him.'

For the next half hour Wicksy could think about nothing else. The idea of a new *identity* had never seriously occurred to him. Nor had the possibility of acquiring one.

Now his brain teemed with possibilities. He didn't have the time to put on weight, but that wasn't necessary. He could shave his head, or dye his hair; he could wear a false moustache until a real one grew; he could wear shades all the time, like a lot of men did; he knew a way to produce convincing-looking scars using rubber cement – he could even give himself a hare lip like the clown he'd had a run-in with that morning. There were tons of possibilities, he decided. Anybody could change his appearance, all it took was a bit of thought.

Back at Geoff's place that afternoon Wicksy recounted the tale of the man who had disappeared. Old Desmond listened, amused, then boosted Wicksy's enthusiasm another couple of notches by telling a story of his own.

'This chap I first met in 1940, he was a deserter from the Army. Fascinating man, very gifted, with no interest at all in getting himself shot to pieces in a war he'd never wanted. He didn't like hiding, either – he was a gregarious type and liked being out and about. So he sat down and thought things over and decided that he'd have to undergo a total change of identity. *But*, he would make a thorough job of it, not one of the usual half-hearted, unimaginative efforts that kept getting deserters caught all over the place.'

'What was it they used to do?' Wicksy asked, keen to learn from other people's blunders.

'Oh . . .' Desmond put back his head and closed his eyes for a minute. 'They falsified their papers, and did it themselves instead of getting hold of an expert, which was easy enough through the black market networks. Or they would get rid of anything that identified them as whoever they were, which usually meant they wound up in prison while lengthy enquiries established their identity. Others

119

took to staying indoors and hiding in lofts or hollowed out furniture like chests of drawers and sideboards – the kind of existence that was worse than any amount of imprisonment, because they had to dive for cover every time somebody came to the door. All very fatuous stuff,' Desmond concluded. 'Hopelessly uninspired.'

'So what did he do, this man you knew?'

'He altered his appearance,' Desmond said. 'Put on about fifteen years by taking out his false teeth. Changed the colour of his hair. *Stopped* wearing glasses in public and got himself a pair of personality lifts at a theatrical supplier's – they put more than three inches on his height, and he soon got over the discomfort of wearing them in his boots. But he did more than that. He got a forged identity card, which was easy enough if you were prepared to lay out some money for it. Then he spent a lot more cash and obtained naval papers in his newly adopted name. To crown it all, he got a petty officer's uniform and wore it everywhere. He behaved openly, drew attention to himself and never sidestepped an approaching policeman.'

'Did he get away with it?'

'Until 1946.' Desmond said. 'Then he changed his identity again and became a Czech film maker, keen on settling in America and pursuing his interrupted career there. The last I heard about him, he was successfully established in the Hollywood community, making television commercials.'

This was heady stuff. Wicksy felt he was on the brink of huge possibilities. He could be free, he could set himself up as anybody. All it took were a few alterations to his appearance and his history. And he could do it as many times as he wanted or needed to.

'I think I'll go for a walk,' he said a few minutes later, while the other two were reading the Sunday papers.

'It looks like it'll rain,' Geoff pointed out.

'That's all right. I like rain.'

He had to get out and think without interruptions. Here was a sound plan, after all. An answer. Wicksy was sure of that. It had to be thought out and practical decisions had to be made, quickly, because time was short.

The rain had started by the time he got outside. The pavements gleamed like waxed silver. In the absence of traffic noise the rhythm of the downpour hissed soothingly on Wicksy's ears. He stepped into the doorway of a closed shop and stood gazing at the top of sooty plane trees in a public garden across the way.

Check this thing out, he thought.

His feelings were a reliable guide. The day hadn't started well: he'd hoped to draw some kind of reassurance from old Todd, but got nothing more than a confirmation that he was in the kind of trouble no man could weather without serious loss. Then he'd been further unsettled when the idiot with one ear and a zigzag lip tried to assault him. That had been the first part of the day, Wicksy decided, and thought of Todd's book-keeping. The first part of the day had been the debit part. It was logical that the remainder should be on the credit side. That was how he felt. He was sure he wasn't kidding himself. He had been handed a brilliant idea by Jacko and it had been hardened into ambition by Desmond's story.

So how would he go about turning himself into somebody else?

He could begin with the hair. Bleaching it would make a radical change in his appearance. Bleached *and* cut short, it would transform him. Then a false moustache – Geoff had some among his collection of movie odds and ends and Wicksy was sure he wouldn't mind parting with one. Then there were the shades – he could buy a pair first thing in the morning.

What else?

A total change, he supposed, would rely on him looking exactly the opposite of who he was, of the kind of person he was. Which meant the clothes would have to be changed. Which wouldn't be easy.

He thought and thought, hearing the rain get heavier. Then it clicked. What he needed was a really square suit, maybe with flared trousers. He could get one at Oxfam, and if they didn't have one he was sure they'd have something staid enough to conceal the fact that the wearer was the freewheeling, sharp-as-they-come Simon Wicks.

He closed his eyes, trying to picture how he would look. He reckoned it was perfect. He wouldn't want to go around looking like that for good; it would serve him, though, while he took time to dream up another, cooler transformation.

He heard a car approach and opened his eyes. His heart began to thump as he watched it slow down. It was the green Toyota saloon. It stopped in the middle of the road. Behind the rain-streaked side window he saw Bryce turn his head and look straight at him. There was no smile, no frown. Just the look, straight-featured and uncompromising. Wicksy nodded. Bryce went on looking at him for another couple of seconds, then he drove on.

Wicksy felt the rain strike his face as the wind changed direction. It was uncomfortable, but nothing to the way he felt inside.

It won't work, he thought. No amount of disguise would help him. Not when he was up against the likes of Benson and Bryce. They saw past everything. They could look into any man and get the measure of who and what he was. Wicksy had felt Bryce's eyes go right into him then and cancel all hope of escape.

He stepped out of the doorway and began walking back to Geoff's place, letting the rain soak him, feeling something like a clammy hand move across his heart.

Ian Bryce hated working on Sundays. He had a wife at home, a good quiet woman who looked after him, didn't argue back and never asked him where he went or what he did. She was worth gold, he'd often thought, especially when a man considered the climate of moral bankruptcy people lived in nowadays. That rainy afternoon he would far rather have been in the house with Bella, sitting in front of the fire, half-sleeping while she was in the kitchen, getting his dinner ready.

But there was work to be done. Strictly speaking it didn't have to be done today, but Ian believed nothing should be deferred if it could be tackled straight away. Besides that, Sunday put the element of surprise at his disposal.

As he headed for Fulham his mind drifted across the priorities of the coming week. He was always on top of the job, but it didn't hurt to run regular checks and look for possible areas of difficulty. In the legitimate world of business Ian Bryce would have occupied a position of utmost trust and responsibility, just as he did in the illegitimate business he was engaged in; he had a sound analytical mind, made quick and positive decisions, always considered the risks before he made a move, and he looked after the boss's interests as if they were his own.

As usual he foresaw no problems over the next six-day period. Everything in the operation of the moneylending side – his special concern – was geared to work well. The mugs stayed in line for the most part, collections were made efficiently and quickly, and the projected percentage increase in the annual rate of profit was usually exceeded. Most important of all, nothing was out of hand. Bryce couldn't tolerate anything getting out of hand.

He thought of young Simon Wicks, remembered the look of him five minutes earlier, standing in the doorway with his eyes shut. What had that been all about? Maybe he'd been composing a tune. The look changed when he had seen the car and its driver. What had that been, that look? Shock, certainly, but something else, something that hinted at disappointment, moving to a kind of despair.

Bryce was ninety percent sure Simon Wicks couldn't meet the payment by noon tomorrow. He would wait and see, though. People developed surprising ingenuity sometimes, given enough pressure. Simon Wicks wasn't the type to get spectacular ingenuity, but even the most clueless individual could occasionally pull a rabbit out of the hat.

Now Bryce thought of Wicks's mother and his tongue moved with distaste. Not many people would have guessed she was the mother of a fine-looking lad like that. She was the kind that used to drink in the few Glasgow pubs that tolerated female clientele in the old days, the days before the rules went soft and anybody was allowed in anywhere. She was a big fat bachle. A seedy shag bag. The kind of strumpet that made a man like Bryce feel his stomach shift when he watched her doing her come-on routine. Simon Wicks had had a bad start, his mother was proof of that. He either had a lot of character to turn out the way he had, or he'd inherited some special resilience from his father. Bryce hoped the lad hadn't inherited any of the treachery that was stamped all over his mother's character. That kind of inheritance could only cause him trouble, and he might be in enough of that already.

As he got closer to Fulham Bryce shifted his attention

to the matter in hand. He had memorized the address and remembered what Marsden had told him: this target fancied himself as a hard case. Marsden, quite rightly, had resisted proving otherwise until he had checked with Bryce, and when Bryce had listened to the story he decided it was a job he should handle himself. It was the kind of case that needed to be dealt with efficiently and swiftly, because there was no profit in it.

At Bel Brook Common he parked the car, crossed the road and took a left turn, then a right. He found himself on a faceless road of Victorian houses. One of them, he knew, would have a brand new door that Marsden had said looked right out of place. Sure enough, halfway along the road was a grey-brown housefront with a cheaply cheerful DIY Edwardian-look, lacquered teak-veneer door with gleaming brass knob, knocker and letterbox. Bryce went along the short path, looked up and down the quiet road for a couple of seconds, then knocked on the door.

A woman came. She was in her thirties, dark-haired and attractive, wearing a shiny kitchen apron that said, YOU NAME IT – I'LL COOK IT. She tilted her head at Bryce, pleasantly inviting him to state his business.

'Mrs Drummond?'

She nodded.

'I wonder is your husband in?'

'Yes. Hang on.'

So trusting, Bryce thought as she went back along the hall. It had a lot to do with his conservative appearance, of course. He had a strong air of respectability and believed, indeed, that he was a respectable man, because he conducted himself in accordance with a strict set of rules.

The man came along the hall slowly, the imposing approach of a person who held himself to be special. He drew back the door and Bryce saw a strong-featured face, a wide frame and black-haired arms, their thickness emphasized by rolled-back shirtsleeves.

'Yes? Can I help you?'

'Derek Drummond?'

'That's me.'

'I'm here on a matter a colleague spoke to you about recently,' Bryce said, sounding like a Scottish insurance agent. 'I believe there was some misunderstanding at the time. I want to clear all that up.'

'What are you talkin' about?' Drummond demanded, his eyes showing that he knew perfectly well.

'A gentleman who works at Gibson's Garage in Ilford – you owe him money, a hundred pounds to be exact. He's pressed you for repayment, I understand. But you've refused. In fact I believe you deny you ever borrowed the money in the first place.'

'Just who are you?' Drummond asked, spreading his feet a fraction and folding his arms.

'Who I am doesny matter, Mr Drummond – '

'But you think that comin' on with the heavy Jock accent an' the cool killer's eyes is goin' to put the frighteners on me, don't you?' Drummond leaned forward a fraction from the hips. 'I told your mate an' now I'm tellin' you – I don't owe any guy in any garage, an' that's that. An' one more thing.' Drummond's arms unfolded, so that he could point a finger at Bryce's chest. 'Any more visits on this matter, from you or your pal or whoever, an' somebody gets to go home with his windpipe in his pocket.'

'That's a very unhelpful attitude,' Bryce said, his voice almost sad. 'I don't think you realize how seriously we take this . . .'

Drummond cocked his head and made a tight, irritable smile. 'What is it with you lot, you Jocks, that makes you

126

think you've got some kind of built-in toughness nobody else can match? Do you think you're makin' me feel threatened, or somethin'?' He jerked a thumb at the gate. 'On your bike, before I show you what tough is.'

Bryce sighed and before the sound had died in his throat he had one hand twisted in the fabric of Drummond's shirt, the other on his arm. Jerking back a step and keeping his arms half flexed, he pulled Drummond on to the path and frog-marched him to the corner of the house.

'Now just be quiet and listen, Mister.'

He threw Drummond against the wall. His back slapped on the bricks and air left his lungs with a whistle and a grunt. Bryce did it again, then let go. Drummond stood wheezing, hands on knees, trying to issue a warning with his eyes.

'I'm not going to waste any more time on this,' Bryce said, his tone brisk now. 'So here it is, flat and plain – you give that man back his money, within one week of this date, or you get your skeleton dismantled. Now have you got that?'

Drummond moved with surprising speed. He leapt at Bryce, fists bunched, one of them heading for the chin, the other for the stomach. Bryce stepped aside and his hand flew to Drummond's throat. As the second intended punch flew as wide as the first, Bryce's thumb tightened on the side of Drummond's neck, making him see sparks. His arms flailed, going suddenly weak. He gurgled something.

'That does it,' Bryce said, close to Drummond's ear. 'Now there's going to be no more warnings. When I finish with you you'll not be able to piss without shrieking.'

He released the pressure on Drummond's neck. The man began to slide down the wall. Before he had completed the descent Bryce's right shoe kicked him on the side of the chest. He went down sideways and caught another shoe on the mouth. His head snapped back and cracked on the wall.

'Just remember,' Bryce said, bending close for a moment, 'Nothing's altered. Pay up within the week, or this'll seem like kids' stuff.'

Drummond looked up, wheezing through a mouth welling with blood. His tongue slipped forward a fraction and dislodged two fragments of tooth from his lip. He watched, powerless to move or shield himself, as Bryce adjusted his stance and sent the first sharp kick into the undefended groin. A voice somewhere was howling, like a frightened child's. Drummond thought, without much clarity, that the voice could be his own.

A couple of minutes later Bryce walked back to the front door of the house, supporting the doubled-over Drummond at arms' length, urging him forward in jerks. Mrs Drummond came to the door as her bleeding, shuddering husband was being lowered unceremoniously to the step. She stared at him, a hand flying to her mouth. Then she looked at Bryce, so tidy and unflurried she could scarcely imagine he'd had anything to do with the catastrophe that had visited her husband.

'What happened?' she squeaked.

'He fell.'

Bryce stepped back, nodded curtly at the tableau of agony and concern, and walked off.

When he was in the car he opened the glove compartment, slid his hand into a polythene bag and took out a sugared almond. He looked at it for a moment, admiring the lilac colour, then popped it into his mouth. He managed to keep his liking for sweets under control, but after a job that required any exertion, he always rewarded himself with one.

'Mission accomplished,' he murmured, switching on the engine. 'Beam me up, Bella.'

There would be beef for dinner, because it had been pork last Sunday. Beef, cabbage, carrots, boiled and roasted potatoes. With a thick aromatic gravy. The image didn't contradict or alter the sweet taste in Bryce's mouth. He could separate a notion from the experience of the moment.

He had done it back there at Drummond's. Engaged in the business of inflicting long-term pain, he had simultaneously imagined doing the same to young Simon Wicks, should the need ever arise. Bryce had to admit that he wouldn't be able to stay so detached if it came to doling out punishment to the lad. He wouldn't be soft on him, of course, for that would be a mark of weakness; but he would feel some regret for the sad necessity.

Bryce drove the car away from the kerb, entertaining a rare surge of concern for another human being. Get the money, son, he thought. Get the readies and save me the discomfort of reminding you the rules are the rules. For ever and ever. Amen.

Jacko had been watching the clock since half-past eight. Business had been steady enough, that wasn't what made him impatient to get the bell rung and turn the punters out on to the street. The aggravation tonight was not the size of the crowd he had in, but the quality. It was pillocks' night, one of those inexplicable times when most of the oddballs, cranks, enthusiasts and far-out hobbyists among his broad clientele had seemed to turn up in the pub at the same time.

It was nearly half-past nine now. Already Jacko had been told, by a member of the Campaign for Real Ale, why his beer would never be better than average until he reconsidered his position on gas-assisted pumping. A man who called himself an antique dealer – which meant he had a once-a-week stall on the Portobello Road – pointed out that the collection of dusty toby jugs on the top shelf of the back fitting was worthless, because none of them dated back further than the war. He had added the advice that Jacko should get into Japanese snuff bottles.

Around nine o'clock a couple of computer nuts came and leaned on the counter, letting their beer go flat while they bandied phrases like 'applications programs', 'database commissioning', 'periodic debugging routines', and 'spreadsheet management'. They also blabbed on about pixels, crashing, screen dumps, error trapping, and a whole lot of other topics that left Jacko in the dark; unfortunately, they were discussed with the kind of high-pitched enthusiasm he couldn't ignore.

Other visitors that evening, most of them still sitting about the place, included a pigeon-fancier who had never owned a bird, an amateur conjurer who did card tricks that required his victims to do mathematical calculations, a lay preacher who tried to convince Jacko that although drinking was no sin the selling of liquor was, and a man who collected empty beer cans.

Now, as the minute hand crept with incredible sloth towards twenty-five to ten, the crowning event of a bizarre evening occurred: Pat rolled in on the arm of an Italian-looking man with an extraordinarily wide centre parting in his crinkly black hair.

'Evenin', Jacko,' Pat said, leaning one arm on the bar and wrapping the other around her companion's shoulder. 'I want you to meet a good friend of mine. Enzio, this is Jacko.'

Jacko nodded. 'Nice to meet you,' he said, and frowned.

'Enzio's a chef.'

'Nice.' Jacko fingered a beer mat. 'What can I get you?'

Pat put on a perplexed face, puckering her mouth little-girl fashion, shaking her head.

'You mean you don't want nothin'?'

'Can't make up my mind.' She grinned impishly at Enzio. 'You decide,' she said.

'Geen and tonic?' he suggested.

'Spot on,' Pat said, slapping a hand on the bar. 'I swear, he can figure out my wants better than I can. But that's your continentals for you, eh Jacko?'

'Definitely. An' what's he havin' himself?'

'Don't say it, don't say it!' Pat cut in before Enzio could open his mouth. 'See if I can guess.' She closed her eyes tightly, then opened them dramatically wide, as if she'd had a genuine vision. 'A scotch an' lemonade.' She stared at Enzio. 'Am I right?'

He smiled smoothly, nodding. 'How do you do eet?'

'You're not just sayin' I'm right are you, just to please me?'

Enzio crossed his heart, causing a jewel on his little finger to wink.

'It happens all the time,' Pat told Jacko. 'We seem to be on a kind of special wavelength, him an' me. It just keeps on happenin' – he knows what I'm feelin' like, I pick up his mood. Creepy, when you think about it.'

'It's been a night for oddities,' Jacko mumbled, getting the drinks. When he brought them Enzio had slipped out to the gents, leaving a fiver with Pat.

'How long have you known him, then?'

'I met him today, this lunchtime,' Pat said. 'He's one of the most fascinatin' men I've ever met. Straight up, Jacko, I mean that. He knows about so many things. Not just food, but travel, books, music, all that.'

Getting the change, Jacko wondered if Pat really believed her own patter. This little Italian was just a pickup, one of a long line of uncles Pat had taken home over the years to meet the kids. The way she was going on, anybody would think she'd found her prince at last. Give it a week, Jacko decided; by that time, she'd be referring to Enzio as that stingy little dago with the funny hair.

'Have you seen Simon tonight at all?' Pat asked when Jacko came back with the change.

'Earlier, about half-seven.'

'Did he say where he was goin' later?'

'Home, he said.'

'Oh, he's got somewhere, then. I knew he would.'

'Left your hearth then, has he?' Jacko said. 'He didn't mention anythin' to me about it.'

'Oh yes, yes.' Pat examined her nails. 'It was time, really. A lad can stop too long with his mum. He needs to get out on his own, make his own life.'

'I'll tell you what,' Jacko said, 'the way he looked when he was in here tonight, I'd have said he was right sick of the life he's makin' for himself. Never saw him so glum.'

'Oh that's nothin',' Pat said, making a pooh-pooh mouth before she took a gulp from her glass. 'Simon's always been too moody.' She winked coyly at Enzio as he came back to the bar, then returned her attention to Jacko. 'He's inclined to exaggerate his troubles, that boy. Nobody knows that better than me. You just watch, he'll bounce back.'

'I hope so,' Jacko said. 'I don't like my staff havin' troubles.'

'Trouble,' Pat said, scoffing. 'Simon doesn't know what trouble is.'

Monday

October 7th. It didn't look or smell different from any other morning. It *felt* no different, which was a surprise. The day of downfall and ruin, Wicksy's Waterloo, should have had at least a distinct atmosphere, something tense and ominous.

Maybe that kind of stuff, he figured, had belonged to the days leading up to this time; travelling could be more exciting – or, in this case, depressing – than arriving.

He sat in the park where he had walked the previous morning with Todd Rumbold. It wasn't quite nine o'clock. He had been out since eight. After thanking Geoff and Desmond for giving him a couple of nights' shelter, and assuring them he was fixed up now, he took his bags to the car, which was tucked away in a back street, and packed them in the boot. He had gone to a café that opened early for the office and factory workers' trade and had a good breakfast, as any condemned man should.

It was cold, with a threat of more rain. Wicksy had his windcheater zipped to the throat and the collar turned up. He sat with a folded newspaper between himself and the bench. The night before he had fallen asleep thinking over his plan again, the one that Todd had said might work, or might go desperately wrong. It had been abandoned when Wicksy got so excited about the possibility of adopting a new identity, but now it had been re-adopted, tentatively, since it offered the only avenue open to him. Last night and this morning he had been asking himself the same question: did he have the guts to take that avenue?

He still wasn't sure. What he had to do, to muster the guts, was to try imagining what would happen if he didn't at least try to carry out his plan. It was hard to do that, to really picture the worst that could take place. His mind kept veering away, frightened by the images.

Now he forced himself, hard, sitting with hands clenched, staring out across the green expanse of parkland without seeing it.

He pictured the rendezvous, a pub, hung with pictures that were nice enough, but symbolic nowadays of the pressure he was under. The place was never busy on a Monday. There would just be himself and a few of the desultory unemployed.

Benson's policy of making collections on a Monday was interesting; it showed the cold, pragmatic nature of his thinking. Most other loan sharks collected on Thursdays and Fridays, getting their hands on the money as soon as it was available. Benson preferred Mondays because, although there was more chance that a man might over-spend at the weekend and find himself short on the day of reckoning, there were nevertheless clear advantages in the arrangement. On a Monday there was less likelihood of heavy human traffic to obscure the absence of this or that individual; Mondays also made it harder for the police to plant plainclothes observers. Above all, Monday was a day when nobody expected the sharks to be making collections, and being fewer on the ground at that time of the week, they were harder to spot.

Wicksy fixed his mind tightly on the scene. He would be standing at the end of the bar, complying with the arrangement, waiting for whichever collector had been appointed to the job that day. He already knew, of course, that it would be Bryce this time.

Bryce. The man's name was enough to make Wicksy sick with foreboding. He was a man with the kind of calm, reptilian malice that certain actors thought they conveyed in the movies. They came nowhere near. The real thing couldn't be faked, it was compactly and frighteningly itself, miles beyond imitation.

Wicksy pictured Bryce coming in, walking up to the bar, ordering a drink. Then he would turn, acknowledge Wicksy with a nod, then stand in such a way that money could be put in his hand without anyone seeing.

Now came the hard part. Wicksy set his teeth as he imagined himself explaining, in a half-whisper, that a snag had developed and he didn't have the cash.

He saw Bryce's face change a fraction. His eyes hardened, turned to chips of basalt. The jaw moved and the question was asked in a snake-whisper – *How soon can you get it?* Wicksy heard himself explain that, as things stood, he had no idea when or how he could ever lay hands on the kind of money he was expected to cough up.

So what are you going to do?

Time, Wicksy said, time would be needed. Time to plan, to put himself in order.

But the meter's running. Time makes interest build up.

Then Wicksy could imagine himself speechless. He had no answer to the rockface rigidity of the rules. He'd used up all the flexibility they had on offer. Now that he was deep into the fantasy it was easy to picture Bryce finish his drink, turn and walk out.

Then it would be the waiting. It might not happen today, but if not, it would certainly be tomorrow. He wouldn't be able to hide. A hand would land on his shoulder, maybe as he was getting into his car, the way Bryce had materialized on Saturday night. There would be a moment of limbo, Wicksy knowing now was the time. He imagined himself frozen on the certainty. Then would come the chaos, the hammering, the pain, the loss of faculties that might never return. And through his agony he would hear the promise of more to come, unless . . .

Wicksy found himself up off the bench, gasping softly. It was the closest he'd come to a wide-awake nightmare.

He turned and faced the gates of the park. Now or never, he thought. He was scared enough, at last, to go through with the plan. He started walking, holding one image in his head, the terrible, punitive face of Bryce, his stillness promising the unthinkable.

At ten past nine Inspector Grace took his paper cup of milky coffee to the office he had been grudgingly allowed to use since his secondment to Ilford eighteen months before. It was hardly big enough to be called an office and had once, indeed, been a spacious broom cupboard, before rationalization had seen it re-assigned as a place where bothersome functionaries could be tucked away.

And Inspector Grace was bothersome. He had come from another force as an oblique punishment; what he had been told, indirectly, was that the powers had felt it wise to separate him from the stable of tame constables he had established elsewhere, a group of yes-men and toadies who would carry out irregular orders from the Inspector without thinking twice.

No one had actually proved that Inspector Grace was corrupt; but he was known to be idiosyncratic, and certainly vindictive. He hounded criminals more energetically than he impeded them, he regularly harboured deep suspicions on gossamer-thin evidence, and he found it difficult to keep his personal feelings anywhere but to the forefront, whatever the case in hand. He would be in Ilford until he retired, he supposed. He was as unhappy about that as most other officers in the area. To compensate for his relative isolation he spent his days being as obstructive and awkward as he could.

This morning it would be easy to ruffle feathers. On the desk there was a circular from the Superintendent, asking senior officers to submit recommendations for improving the effectiveness of policing on local housing estates. Grace could write four pages on that topic, and in the process he could lob muck at a half-dozen officers he disliked, and whose views and practices he always disagreed with on principle.

But before that there was the pleasure of a reprimanding, for which Inspector Grace was just in the mood, having had a row with his wife before he came out that morning, and having lost. He looked at his watch, saw he had five minutes yet, and sat sipping his coffee, mentally framing his vitriolic response to the Superintendent's circular. When the cup was drained he sat up straight in his chair, his belly protruding over the edge of the desk, and tapped the bellpush.

A shirtsleeved young policeman came in at once.

'Is Constable Stigmore out there?'

'Yes, sir.'

'Send him in.'

The door closed. Grace touched his tie, flicked his jacket lapels. There was a soft knock.

'Come in.'

Stigmore was in his early twenties, suitably lean and fresh-faced with short wiry hair, an appearance which Grace couldn't help taking as a rebuke to his own balding, near-corpulent middle age.

'I suppose you know why you're here, Constable?'

'Yes sir. It's about my girlfriend.'

Grace nodded, glancing at the notes in front of him.

'I'd like to know who reported me, sir.'

'I beg your pardon?'

'The Sergeant told me yesterday I'd be on the carpet in front of you this morning because I'm going out with

Doris Struthers. I asked him why that was, but he couldn't tell me. He said I'd better ask you, he was just passing on information.'

'I see.' Grace folded his arms, straining the shoulders of his jacket. 'Well, the fact is, Stigmore, nobody reported you. Have you done anything you think you *should* be reported for?'

'No sir, I haven't.'

'I'm relieved to hear it.' Grace stared at the young man, noticing the stillness of his stance, the nervousness. 'You were observed drinking with the young lady in three separate places on three consecutive evenings this week. Observed by *me*, Constable.'

'Might I ask why you've been tailing me, sir?'

'Who said anything about tailing you?'

'With respect,' Stigmore said, 'it seems a bit too much of a coincidence that you should be in the same places we were on those three nights.'

The Inspector glared, his mouth working as if he were chewing a very small piece of gum.

'Are you being insolent?' he demanded.

'No, sir. I just want to know what's been going on. And why?'

'I'm asking the questions!' Grace snapped. 'Now.' He slapped both hands flat on the desk. 'Can you offer me some explanation? An excuse, perhaps?'

Stigmore frowned delicately. 'For what?'

'For keeping company with Doris Struthers, of course. A policeman has to be seen to be above reproach, right? His public behaviour, on and off duty, must be exemplary. Yet you've been flaunting a relationship with the daughter of a known criminal.'

'Mr Struthers isn't a criminal, sir,' Stigmore said, his face reddening.

'What?' Grace did his best to look shocked and bewildered. 'If a convicted murderer isn't a criminal, I don't know what is.'

'Until the time of the killing Mr Struthers led a blameless life.'

'I'm not about to argue about this,' Grace blustered. 'The fact remains – '

'And it wasn't a murder.' Stigmore's voice had begun to waver with emotion, but his eyes were steady. 'Manslaughter, the court decided. Committed at a time when he was under excessive personal pressure. That was why the sentence was so lenient, and it's why he was released from prison after serving the minimum term.'

'I'll thank you not to interrupt me! Or to try fogging matters! You're here because you've chosen to keep company, in public, with the daughter of a man who slaughtered his own wife.'

'In self-defence.'

'Stigmore!' Grace pushed back his chair and stood, hands spread on the desk. He was glaring like a pink bulldog. 'Keep quiet while I'm addressing you! I don't want to have to throw in a charge of insubordination!'

They stared at each other, Stigmore shaking now, the Inspector raw from finding the sure ground not so sure after all.

'You're here to be reprimanded. So I hereby reprimand you, Constable. And I'm ordering you to mend your ways.'

'I don't understand, sir.'

'Stop seeing the girl!'

Stigmore looked at the floor for a second.

'I'm going to register a complaint, sir.'

'You're going to *what*?'

'Register a complaint. Against you.'

'And what grounds would you have for that?'

'I'm being treated unfairly – as far as I know, you've no

right to reprimand me in this matter, or to tell me how I should choose my women friends. I'm planning to marry Doris Struthers, incidentally.'

Grace saw defiance, and seeing it he began to feel very unsure of himself. It wasn't the first time, and it was a feeling he abhorred.

'Get out,' he said.

'Yes, sir.'

As the door closed the Inspector sat down again, feeling he might have blundered. That was odd, damnably odd, because he had been so sure he'd proceeded correctly. What was wrong in tailing a young policeman, especially when there was evidence that he was bringing the force into disrepute? And why shouldn't he be reprimanded and ordered to stop what he was doing?

The questions thudded off the sides of Grace's skull, receiving no satisfactory answers, no rebuttal. Yet he still felt this wouldn't go too well for him.

'Cheeky young bastard,' he growled at the desk, then jerked back in his chair as the door was knocked loudly. 'Yes?'

The door opened and a detective put his head round the edge.

'Could you spare a minute or two, sir?'

'What's the problem?'

'We've got a chap upstairs, he wants some help. He came to CID, but I think it should be you he's talking to.'

Anything to get the taste of Stigmore out of his mouth, Grace thought. He got up and followed the detective up to the CID interview rooms.

'He's in there, sir.' The detective pointed to the third door along the passage. 'I'll be in the office if you want me.'

Grace walked into the interview room without knocking. He looked at the man sitting at the table. Instantly, he was identifying this character with the uniformed one he had just tried to deal with.

'Simon Wicks Esquire.'

Wicksy looked sick.

'I understand you want some help.'

Instead of taking the chair opposite Wicksy, the Inspector leaned on the wall by the door and slipped his hands in his trouser pockets.

'You know, of course, that after our last meeting I'll be only too glad to give you all the help I can.' Grace smiled sourly. 'Shoot, then. Let's hear it.'

'I wanted to talk to the CID,' Wicksy said. 'It's them I came to see – '

'And they obviously decided it's a matter for the uniformed branch.'

'I don't want to talk to you.'

'Fine. Bugger off, then.'

Wicksy knew the plan was likely to hit snags, but he hadn't expected any to develop this early.

'I'd like to talk to your Super,' he said.

'You have to talk to me first. Then I'll tell you if you can talk to him or not.'

Wicksy considered his position. Having scared himself into this course of action, he couldn't imagine not going through with it. He looked at Inspector Grace, hating the half-sneer, the casual authority. He was playing the big man on his own turf, like pub landlords did. Wicksy sighed.

'Right. I'll talk to you.'

'Keep it short.' Grace crossed his ankles. 'I'm a busy man.'

'It's a problem I've got,' Wicksy said, lacing and unlacing his fingers. 'Money.'

'You surprise me,' Grace drawled.

'I got mixed up with moneylenders. Loan sharks. The

heavy kind. For a while I was on top of it, I made the repayments when I should . . .'

'Then you started to find it harder.'

'Yeah.'

'And you missed a payment.'

'That's it. I'd got in over my head.'

'Mugs like you always do.'

One prod on the shoulder, just one, was all it would take to make Wicksy throw himself out of that chair and put one squarely on Grace's nose. And happily take the consequences. That, it occurred to him, might get him safely off the streets for a while. But a time would come when he would have to go back out there. He clenched his jaw for a second and told himself to ignore the needling.

'Anyway,' he said, 'it's got to the point where if I don't meet today's payment, I think I'll get done over. In fact I'm sure I will. It'll be just a warnin', but blokes have got crippled on them kind of warnin's.'

'It's not a new story.'

'I know it ain't,' Wicksy said.

'So why are you tellin' me all this?'

'I had an idea.' Wicksy looked up from his hands, saw the sneer and looked down again. 'I thought that if I was watched – you know, by the police – an' when it happened, when the heavies jumped me – '

'We could pull them in for assault,' Grace said. 'And because that kind don't like any involvement with the police, or with people who're connected with the police for whatever reason, they'd cut their own men loose and stay well clear of you.'

'An' I could testify to the moneylendin' set up. I know who the boss is, an' one or two of his lads.'

'Do you think we don't know?'

Wicksy blinked at the Inspector.

142

'We'd have had them in long ago, on a dozen charges,' Grace said, 'if we could have got a reliable witness.'

'I'd be reliable,' Wicksy said. 'I mean, I don't like grassin', but if it's goin' to save my skin . . .'

'You're a lot thicker than I gave you credit for, Simon.' Grace moved away from the wall and strolled halfway across the room. He stopped and studied the crime-prevention poster on the opposite wall. 'Do you seriously think you'd ever testify against these men? Even on a simple assault charge? Do you imagine they'd let you?'

'But if I got protection . . .'

'For how long? Fifty years strapped to a bobby, is that what you've got in mind? Listen, they'd let you know, swiftly, just how you stand. And they'd reach you wherever you ran to. No man is an island, and the loan sharks of this world certainly aren't. They're linked to networks so devious and complicated it'd make your eyes water trying to work them out.'

'Surely it's worth a try,' Wicksy said, feeling the onset of despair. 'I'm not as chicken as they might think. I'd go into court, straight I would.'

'It's *not* worth a try, take my word for it.' Grace faced Wicksy, folding his arms. 'First off, I don't think you would go into the dock, much as you might think you would. You'd get frightened off. Like you are now, comin' here with your crazy plan. It's not a plan, it's a dream. And like most dreams it's nonsense. Even if you did, by some miracle, find yourself capable of getting up and blowing the whistle on the baddies, you'd only be putting yourself in deeper trouble. See it straight. They'd crucify you.'

'Listen . . .' Wicksy swallowed nervously. He was getting desperate. 'How can you know it won't work? Why not give it a try?'

'It's been tried,' Grace said flatly. 'Men have come

143

forward, prepared to set themselves up as decoys. Hard men some of them, determined to have a bit of revenge. But they've all folded before we even had a case put together. Always.'

The last feeble strands of Wicksy's faith in his plan broke suddenly. He should have known it, he should have realized he'd thought of nothing new or workable. Todd should have known, too, and should have warned him not even to try. Wicksy dismissed that bitter thought almost as soon as it came to him, realizing that Todd's knowledge of the loan sharks' world dated from a time of relative innocence, if no less brutality. He looked at Grace.

'So what can I do?'

'I've no idea. What you can't do, though, is speak to my Superintendent.' Grace smiled briefly. 'Permission denied. He's too busy to listen to master plans that come straight out of the Beezer.'

'That's it? I don't get any help at all?'

'You've put yourself beyond the reach of our help. And frankly, I wouldn't be inclined to give the likes of you any help, even if I could.' The Inspector jerked his thumb at the door. 'You can go now. Back out into the big cruel world. Or would you maybe like to talk to your step-father? He's still here.'

'Keep him,' Wicksy said, getting up and walking to the door.

'Simon.'

Wicksy paused in the corridor. 'Yeah?'

'You're a loser. A loser bred of losers. Give in to it. Swimming against the tide's no good. Your kind always go under, so it might as well be sooner as later.'

'Cheers.'

Grace watched the empty doorway for a minute, deciding that it had done him some good talking to young Wicks. A score had been settled. The rawness of the experience with Constable Stigmore had been partially soothed. As Monday mornings went, it could have been worse.

When he got to the street Wicksy decided to go and sit in a dark café somewhere. He needed time to get used to the idea that his worst dream, the one he had deliberately put himself through less than an hour ago, was shortly to come true.

He went to the Bay Tree, a greasy spoon that justified its name by having one stunted shrub in a plastic tub by the side of the door.

'Mornin', Wicksy,' the proprietor, Benny, called through the smoky hatch. 'The à la carte ain't on yet, I'm afraid.'

'I'm not hungry, Benny. Just a coffee, please.'

There were no other customers in the place. Wicksy sat down in the cubicle seat furthest from the door. He had his head in his hands when Benny brought the coffee.

'Hangover, is it?'

'No.' Wicksy looked up. 'I'm tryin' to work somethin' out. How to turn invisible.' He had known Benny since he was a little boy and could tell him anything. He smiled briefly at the good-natured, unshaven old face. 'Some bad men are goin' to want my blood soon.'

'God, no . . .' Benny pushed the coffee towards Wicksy and slid into the seat opposite. 'That's desperate. What's the score?'

Wicksy gave him a summary.

'When's the showdown?' Benny asked.

'High noon.'

'You've got time to scarper, then.'

'I can't see any future in that. Facin' the music's not a lot better, but I think I might get some kind of peace out of it. If I go on the run, I won't have a minute's peace. An' I'd never be able to come back.' Wicksy tasted the coffee, spooned in some sugar and stirred it. 'An' of course, if I did go on the run, an' they did catch me, I'd get a worse doin' over than the one I ran away from.'

'I suppose that's one way of lookin' at it,' Benny said. 'Personally, I wouldn't be able to think it out like that. I'd be too busy shittin' bricks an' packin' my bags.'

A customer shuffled in. Benny got up, served him and came back to the cubicle, bringing a cup of tea for himself.

'You've got a point there,' he said, leaning close to Wicksy as he sat down. 'About not runnin' or hidin', I mean. I was just thinkin' about a bloke that lived near me, must have been back in the early 'sixties I suppose. He got in deep with the lenders. He suddenly went missin', owin' them a couple of hundred or so. They hung around a long time, askin' his wife if she'd heard from him, keepin' an eye on his house an' the pubs he used, all that stuff. Nobody had any idea where he'd gone. Then one mornin', it must have been a year after he vanished, we saw an ambulance outside his house.' Benny shook his head at the memory. 'Poor bugger.'

'What happened?'

'He'd been hidin' in the house all along. In a cupboard. His missus spilled the whole story at the inquest. Every time there was a knock at the door, or when his wife went out to the shops, or the kids came in from school, he had to get in the cupboard. Can you imagine it? Even his kids didn't know he was in the house. At nights he'd sit in the dark, waitin' for the nippers' bedtime, then he'd creep out, have a couple of hours by the fireside with the curtains drawn tight an' the doors locked, then he'd go to bed an' get up early, so he could be in the cupboard again before the kids were up an' about.'

'He spent a year like that.'

Benny nodded. 'An' the prospect, I suppose, was that he'd always have to live that way. So one mornin' he took

146

a razor blade into the cupboard with him. Probably sat an' thought about it for a while, reckoned it was hopeless. When his wife tapped the door to let him know he could slip out for a cuppa, he didn't answer. So she opened the door and there he was, lyin' on the floor in a puddle of blood. He'd cut his throat. Dead on arrival at the hospital. It's hard to imagine the kind of hell that bloke went through before he topped himself.'

Wicksy groaned over the lip of his coffee cup.

'I'm sorry,' Benny said. 'I didn't mean to depress you, son.'

'I can't get any more depressed. I was just thinkin' about another story I heard, about deserters durin' the war, hidin' in lofts an' hollow furniture an' all sorts. They must have had a pretty bad time of it, too.'

'Yeah. But at least they got an amnesty. Moneylenders don't hand out amnesties. The best they do, once in a blue moon, is let people off the hook. After they've tortured them an' bloody near killed them.'

Wicksy drained his cup. 'I've been hearin' an awful lot of stories lately,' he said. 'Maybe somethin' about me invites them. It's as if I'm bein' told that unless I turn into the world's greatest expert in disguise, the best I could do is what the guy in the cupboard did.'

Benny looked at him carefully for a couple of seconds.

'You wouldn't think of doin' anythin' like that, would you?'

'No, I wouldn't. I'm too curious, Benny. I want to know what's goin' to happen next, even when I'm pretty sure I know what it is, an' how terrible it's goin' to be. Suicide's not in my make-up.'

'I'm glad to hear it.'

'Mind you, I might feel different about that in a couple of hours.' Wicksy stood up. 'I'll pay you an' clear off, Benny. I'm sure you've had enough of my gloom.'

'The coffee's on me,' Benny said. He rose and slapped Wicksy's shoulder. 'Best of luck, mate.'

Wicksy walked to where his car was parked, checked that it hadn't been burgled or vandalized, then set off northwards on an impulse he felt too low to analyse.

In less than twenty minutes he was at the rear of a vacant lot, beside a crumbling wall. It came as high as his shoulder, but when he had first climbed it he had needed to be helped up by a couple of his little pals. Now Wicksy looked over the wall and saw a familiar tangle of stunted trees and thick tufted grass – familiar even though he hadn't been there for at least ten years.

He put his hands on the top and pulled himself up, swung his legs over and jumped down on the other side. The ground was damp and spongy, rising steeply towards a derelict and half-demolished electricity sub-station that had been out of action since the 'fifties. Wicksy ducked low and elbowed his way through tree branches, remembering how they had once cleared his head as he made his way up the incline.

He stopped in front of the old red-brick building, remembering its layout, knowing that under the rusty sheet of steel in the far right corner was a small chamber where a maximum of four small lads could crouch in reasonable comfort, pretending they were in a spaceship, or any kind of craft they fancied.

Wicksy stepped inside, knowing suddenly why he had come. For years, roughly between the time he was six until he was about nine or ten, he had run to this place to experience freedom and safety. This had been the escape and sanctuary of childhood.

The steel plate had flaked badly at the edges and its handle broke off in his hand as he reached down to shift it. Carefully he wrapped his fingers round the edges and slid the plate to one side.

148

Nostalgia was powerful as he stepped down into the chamber, wondering at how small it really was; standing up straight, he was head and shoulders above the edge. At one time it was a scary leap down and a scramble back up again. Without feeling in the least silly, Wicksy crouched and eased himself back into a corner.

They had sat hushed in here, their warm breath mingling as alien soldiers searched for them in the jungle outside. At other times they had piloted a ship towards a smoky planet, clung tight as their submarine tilted, made whispered plans to break from cover suddenly and overwhelm an entire encampment of Germans. This place had been whatever Wicksy and his pals wanted it to be. And it had always been the safest hideout in the world.

It was heartbreakingly true; there had been a time when secure retreat was possible. There had been a secret world, an alternative to his mother's temper or the big boys' bullying.

He stood up again and looked around. Wonderland was only a dead building, an inert husk now there were no innocent dreams to give it life. Bereft of his childhood, Wicksy knew he brought nothing here; the place, in its turn, could impart nothing to him. But it had been nice to come back and remember how good a childhood he'd had, at times. And how safe, when he wanted it to be.

At five minutes to twelve he walked into the appointed pub, bought a Coke and stood with his hands around it, waiting. No one took any notice of him standing there. To everyone he was anonymous. But he felt conspicuous, vulnerable. His stomach churned so badly he didn't dare try to swallow any of his drink.

When Bryce arrived Wicksy felt him before he saw him. He was an electric presence moving up on the left, the only truly integrated person in the room. He stood beside Wicksy, more or less as he had in the fantasy.

'Hello there, Simon.'

'Mr Bryce.'

To anyone watching, the exchange would have seemed perfectly ordinary. Two acquaintances had met, probably by accident. There was no outward hint of impending nemesis.

Bryce ordered a scotch, paid for it and took a sip.

'Well now, Simon,' he said, without looking at Wicksy. 'Do you have the necessary?'

'I'm afraid not.'

No change in Bryce. He sipped again, put down his glass on the polished bar.

'What went wrong?'

'Everything.' Wicksy's fingers tightened around his glass. 'The fact is, I couldn't raise it. I've nobody an' no place to get it from.'

Bryce exhaled audibly. It was the sound of authority impelled, reluctantly, to a last resort.

'You know the consequences?'

'I've thought about nothin' else.'

'And thinking about it's done nothing for your, ah, ingenuity?'

'Honestly,' Wicksy said, 'I haven't a bean an' I can't raise the kind of money that's needed.'

'So you think the best thing is to tell me, and I'll be swayed by your honesty and your natural charm and write the debt off to experience. Is that what you think?'

'I don't think anythin' I say is goin' to make any difference. But tellin' you was all I could do.'

Bryce raised his glass, looked at it, then tipped the remainder of the whisky down his throat. The glass touched the bar with a click. He turned, looking straight at Wicksy.

'I can tell you this. I was wishing you'd come up with the goods. Wishing not just because of the debt itself, but

150

because of you, too. Do ye understand what I'm saying?'

Wicksy nodded. 'I think so.'

'Ah can't change the rules, Simon. Don't want to, as it happens. But I'm sorry about this, as sorry as my principles can let me be.'

Bryce turned, buttoning his raincoat, and left the pub.

Wicksy stayed where he was, still holding the glass of Coke for support.

I've done it. I've told him.

While the sense of relief lasted he would relish it. He picked up the glass and took a mouthful. His hand shook so badly the rim of the tumbler rattled on his teeth. The bad time was still to come, of course. But clearing that hurdle, actually turning up and levelling with Bryce, had scored him some points with himself. For the first time in ages Wicksy began to feel he was somebody, after all.

The rain started at ten past three, bang on cue for the exodus from the Ginger Giant. As men grumbled their way out on to the street Jacko went round picking up glasses, expressing sporadic sympathy for the victims of licensing laws that cast him in the rôle of a heartless swine, insisting his customers leave at once, the torrent notwithstanding.

As the last punter but one went out Jacko dumped eight pint glasses on the bar, disentangled his fingers from their necks and turned to Wicksy, who had been leaning on the wall by the window for more than an hour.

'The trouble with you is,' Jacko said, 'you're in love with the sound of your own voice.'

Wicksy shrugged and pushed himself away from the wall with his elbow.

'I've nothin' much to say, Jacko.'

'I'd have sworn you were a statue of yourself, if I hadn't seen your head movin' a couple of times. An' you're a better barman than you are a customer. A half pint's all you've had, an' you left a bit in the bottom of that.' Jacko stepped closer and put his hands on his hips. 'What's the matter, eh?'

'I've been ponderin' about things.'

'What kind of things.'

'Oh, it's hard to explain.' Wicksy picked up the remaining three uncollected glasses and put them on the bar. 'Three hours ago, I'd have said I'd a pretty good idea how my future would go.'

'That's more than most folk would know.'

'Most people don't have it mapped out for them like I have,' Wicksy said. 'The thing is, I'm gettin' the feelin' now that I shouldn't just let things happen to me.'

Jacko screwed up his eyes, appealing for clarity.

'That's a mistake I've been makin', Jacko. I've made arguments against doin' the right thing. They were good arguments, good enough to make me think it was the wrong thing.'

'I haven't a clue what you're talkin' about.'

'It doesn't matter,' Wicksy said, heading for the door. 'I'll be seein' you. Be good.'

The soaked world outside the pub felt desperately dangerous now. Wicksy zipped up and put his head down, running at a trot down the alley and on to the main road. He waited for the traffic to thin then darted across the road and into an Indian clothing store.

'Can I help you, please?' the lady behind the counter said.

'I want a woolly hat. The balaclava kind, you know?'

The woman nodded, looking out at the weather.

'I have waterproof hats,' she pointed out. 'They are cheaper than the woollies, too.'

'No. It's the woolly kind I want. Black, if you have it.'

The woman fumbled through a box and produced a

dark grey balaclava, the closest she had to black. Wicksy put it on and looked at himself in the mirror by the door. He decided he looked like a wally.

'I'll take it, thanks.'

At least, he thought as he went out, he didn't look like Simon Wicks any more. Not unless somebody got close and had a really good look.

He felt safer now, though not safe. He kept his face turned down as he trotted through the puddles back to the Bay Tree. Benny was mopping the counter. He looked up for an instant but registered no recognition.

'How soon we forget,' Wicksy said.

Benny looked again, came close and peered.

'Bloody hell, it's you, Wicksy. You look a right poultice with that thing on.'

'As long as I don't look like who I usually look like, I don't mind. Coffee please, Benny. An' I think I'll have a burger in a bun, to keep my strength up.'

Benny nodded, but didn't move.

'Tell me then,' he said.

'Oh. I did it. I told the guy. No bread, sorry an' all that.'

'An' he let you off?'

'No,' Wicksy said, 'he didn't do that. I'm up for the high jump, he made it plain enough.'

'He didn't try anythin' there an' then?'

'It's not the style nowadays, Benny. They make you wait. The waitin's part of the punishment.'

When the coffee and burger were ready Benny brought them to the cavernous corner where Wicksy had sat earlier. As before Benny sidled in opposite with a mug of tea.

'I'm surprised you can eat,' he said, watching Wicksy bite a chunk out of the burger. 'If I'd anythin' hangin' over me like you've got, I couldn't get a crumb past me lips without gaggin'.'

'I'm eatin',' Wicksy said through the mouthful, 'because my head's unscrambled itself. I always get peckish when I've got my act together.'

'What does that mean?'

'I'm takin' off. Runnin'. Like just about everybody's told me to do.'

'But you said you'd decided against that. You practically convinced me it was best to stay an' take your medicine.'

Wicksy took another bite from the bun, nodding, waving a hand to fill the gap until he could speak again.

'That argument was the result of thinkin' ahead,' he said finally. 'But what I didn't take account of was this – I always got my best results by actin' on my strongest impulse.'

'Well . . .' Benny turned down the corners of his mouth, a sign of severe doubt. 'You borrowed that money on a bit of an impulse, didn't you?'

'Not the same kind,' Wicksy said. 'I don't want to start makin' out this is deep stuff. What I'm sayin' is, after I'd talked to that guy today I began to feel quite good. I got a bit of my self-respect back, because I'd faced the music. Or that part of the music, anyway. I perked up enough to decide I don't want to give in. I'd sooner go down fightin'.' He eased a piece of bread from his teeth and chewed it thoughtfully. 'I've only realized today what a pratt I've been these past few weeks. See, I reckoned I'd no real choice but to give in. All the alternatives fell through. Except one – runnin'. But I hated the idea of that, I was sure it'd be terrible, a nightmare. But I don't know it'll be so bad, do I?'

'You don't know it won't be, either,' Benny said.

'That's true. But fortune don't help anybody that don't

help himself, right? So I'm at least goin' to try gettin' out of this.'

'Like I told you before,' Benny said, sighing, 'best of luck.'

'Cheers, mate. I reckon I'll have another burger.'

In the hour before it got dark, Wicksy had time to stand back from what he was doing and see if he truly agreed with his own actions. He decided, as he approached the street where his car was parked, that his reasoning, as he had put it to Benny, was only partly sound. It was what he *hadn't* told Benny – something which was gut feeling, not reasoning – that made him determined to run, and to do it tonight.

The street was secluded, but it was uncomfortably well lit. Wicksy walked past the end once, with his balaclava in position, and fancied he saw somebody standing on the pavement near the car. He passed again and he was sure of it, except the man wasn't standing there; he was walking a few yards past the car in one direction, then turning and doing the same the opposite way. And there was another man, doing the stroll-and-turn routine on the opposite side of the street.

A clear plan of campaign, Wicksy decided. They were grounding him, making sure he was without wheels. And if he was daft enough to try snatching the car from under their noses, he'd get his comeuppance there and then.

So let them get cold, Wicksy thought. He would go and have a drink, stay among people in a brightly lit place for a while. But he would come back. Having decided he wanted elbow room, he wasn't going to change his mind because a couple of goons were standing guard over his car.

He went to the Thornton and from a corner of the crowded lounge he watched his mother making a fool of herself with a little man who looked like an Italian. She was sitting on his knee, dwarfing him, alternately whispering suggestively in his ear and gulping from her whisky glass.

For once Wicksy felt detached from the woman. She meant nothing to him, and for the moment he didn't even think of the woman buried within her, the one who could move him to sympathy. He saw a gross, loud, completely unlovely woman, self-destructive to a degree that was morally criminal, prepared to disport herself with any man who had the price of an evening's drink on him. Perhaps it was because he was determined to leave this place forever – Wicksy wasn't sure – but tonight Pat seemed like a feature of a long dead past.

So did other people he saw, though not all of them. With a small pang he spied Beckie, sitting at the bar, gushing to a man who looked about forty. Beckie, Beckie, he thought; if only he'd been able to give her the little attention she needed, they might have become something more, to each other, than good-looking escorts. But life for Simon Wicks, so far, had been full of 'if only'. That was something he would have to work on, if he ever had the chance. He tore his eyes away from Beckie and looked at the clock. Soon, he promised himself. Soon.

He left the Thornton at the same time as a dozen or so young people, deliberately positioning himself at the centre of the small crowd and moving with them, keeping their cover to the end of the road.

He took a couple of shortcuts, his scalp and face itching from the damp balaclava. When he got to the end of the street where his car sat forlornly under the street lamps, the men had gone.

Wicksy waited in the shadows, watching. After a minute he saw both of them. They were leaning on a wall, talking, tucked back from prominent view between two overhanging garden trees. Wicksy estimated they were ten yards from the car, on the opposite side of the road. Not far enough. But when was enough ever granted? Wicksy would have to make do. Or go down trying.

His preparations were careful. He pulled the chin of the balaclava up over his mouth, the top down until it touched his eyebrows. He took the car keys from the short chain attached to his belt, then detached the chain and wrapped it round the knuckles of his left hand. In his right hand he took a tight grip on the key that opened the car and operated the ignition, holding it ready for use. Then he began walking.

The men saw him when he was five yards away from the car. They were alert to his presence, though not to an extent that suggested they were suspicious. Wicksy walked on with his eyes down, adjusting the angle of the key. As he drew alongside the car he stopped and looked across the road, at a point several yards beyond the place where the men leaned. They looked where he was looking and he shoved the key into the door lock. By the time they looked back at him he was pulling the door open.

He was halfway into the car before they reacted. They ran across the road, one going in front of the car, the other behind. Wicksy had the door nearly shut when it was jerked open again. A big ugly head came into the car and Wicksy punched it with his left fist, jarring the chain on the man's teeth. He fell back, striking the second man and knocking him over.

'Oi!' The second man had his hand on the edge of the door. 'Get out of there, bastard features!' He struggled up past his wounded mate and drew himself halfway into the car as Wicksy fired the engine. 'Out, you little shit!'

Wicksy leaned back, as if he was avoiding the man, then he came forward at speed. His forehead struck the heavy between the eyes, crunching something. He grunted and fell sideways. Wicksy threw the engine into gear and tore away from the kerb, leaving the door flapping open. At the far end of the street he braked, slammed the door shut and looked behind him. The two men were still on the ground.

Heading for Waterloo, keeping his speed under the limit, observing all the rules, Wicksy realized that he'd really burned his boats now. In style. There was no going back, no reasonable hope of leniency if they ever caught up with him. Oddly, the enormity of what he had done didn't touch him. All he felt was freedom, and that left no room for anything else.

His plans were laid. He would park the car in Waterloo and sleep in it overnight. In the morning he would go into the railway station with one of his bags, have a good wash and shave and change into some decent clothes.

Then he would drive to the London borough of Walford, to the bosom of his real dad. Wicksy had no idea what reception he would get, but he would do all he could to make Pete Beale like him and be proud of how he had turned out.

Walford wasn't so far away. He wasn't putting himself beyond the long reach of the loan sharks. But that wasn't the point.

The point of the exercise was the part he hadn't told Benny. If Benson's boys did catch up with him in Walford, they would catch him in a place where, with luck, his family would be concerned for him. And would defend him.

That was really something, Wicksy thought, smiling. It was certainly tons more than he'd ever have going for him in Ilford.